I0642684

IM PRESS

ALEXANDER SIROTIN-LACHMAN

FROM SOMEWHERE OVER THERE TO SOMEWHERE OVER HERE

Short stories collection

Edited by Anna Tucker

BOSTON · 2025

ALEXANDER SIROTIN-LACHMAN
From Somewhere Over There to Somewhere Over Here
Collection of Short Stories
Edited by Anna Tucker

ISBN 978-1960533715 (pbk)

Published by M·GRAPHICS | BOSTON, MA
✉ mgraphics.books@gmail.com
💻 mgraphics-books.com

Book Design by Yulia Timoshenko © 2025
Cover Design by Larysa Studinskaya © 2025
Photography by Alexander Sirotin-Lachman © 2024

Cover illustration based on *The Vladimirka* (1892) by Isaac Levitan. Tretyakov Gallery, Moscow. Public Domain.

Printed in the U.S.A.

Table of Contents

Foreword

...Aparticularly poignant piece by Alexander Sirotin, a Moscow-born actor, director, and writer,
deals with those Soviet émigrés who, finding it hard to
adjust to life in the United States, yearn for the life they
knew in Russia. "Some long for Kiev, forgetting their own
and others' misery there. Others dream about Leningrad,
because what was bad is easily forgotten. We forget that
we were sitting on a powder keg. We forget that at any
time they could frame another Jewish doctors' case. They
could declare mobilization, evacuation, expropriation,
anything." Sirotin offers this advice to his fellow émigrés:
"Fall in love with Forest Hills and Brighton Beach. Fall
in love with the velvety Manhattan. Fall in love with the
night bridge across the Universe. Fall in love with multicolored girls on multicolored streets. Fall in love with this
great country. It is yours, it is for you. It has stretched out
its hand. Stretch out yours."

Murray Polner,
editor of the *Present Tense* magazine published
by the American Jewish Committee.

Author's Foreword

This book is a collection of stories written in various genres, at various times and in various countries. Some were born in the early 1970s in Moscow. These tales reflect the author's realization of his imprisonment and the absurdity of the country that was building its version of communism. In 1976, the final decision to escape the Soviet Union and run as far as possible, was made. "As far as possible" was the USA, where my mother, a former actress of the Moscow State Jewish Theater, and myself arrived in February of 1979. My observations of immigrants from communist countries to their new life of free initiative, free enterprise, and personal responsibility provided food for both funny and sad monologues, as well as contemplations of my own place in the new country, which I presented in rhythmic prose. Still, even here I had encountered elements of the absurd that, evidently, accompany our lives regardless of place and time.

Through many stories, monologues, and fairytales, runs the theme of the Jewish, and particularly Russian-Jewish, identity with its obvious and underlying burden of centuries of persecution of the Jewish people. The author attempts to tint the humorous monologues with a Jewish accent. Jewish tradition is also reflected in the elements of a parable that the author employs in Sack Race, A Wagon, House of Mirrors, and several others, which come close to being play scripts. The Russian identity can be seen in some stories also, especially the ones that include elements of Russian folklore.

A number of true stories describe events that the author either participated in or was a witness to.

Finally, the collection includes two short stories by the author's mother Nechama Sirotina. There are two reasons for this. First, to preserve them in print, Second, to show the continuity of the gift through generations. It is also a respectful bow of the son in remembrance of and gratitude to his mother whose short life was filled with suffering.

"I Trust You, Doctor."

" Look, this is the only way. We have tried every treatment with no positive results. I am sure this new method will be effective."

"But I have already agreed, doctor. Are you trying to convince yourself?"

"Excuse me?"

"Are you trying to convince yourself that I need this surgery?"

"Not at all. I'm just trying to reassure you and help you stay calm."

"I am calm."

Well, that was awkward. She may really think that I'm not convinced that the surgery will go well. I am, though. I am absolutely sure everything will go smoothly.

Her heels drum a cheerful staccato that echoed in the empty stairwell. She does not like elevators. She does not like anything passive. An enclosed box where a person just stands waiting for his or her stop is not for her. She has to hold the steering wheel, do everything herself — quickly, precisely, and confidently. Otherwise nothing in this life can be achieved. And she has to achieve a lot.

"You are a promising student," Anatoly Ivanovich told her one day. After that, the whole class nicknamed her "Promising". And why not? Her graduate paper was an envy of the entire department. She has been assigned the job she wanted. Now, she has to defend her PhD thesis, and she has high hopes for it.

She pictures a vast banquet hall. Everyone will be drinking the health of the newly made PhD in medical science Irina Yakovlevna Vorontsova. "Can you believe it? Irina is already an MD!" her college friends will marvel. And to him, she will say quietly: "Now we can do it." Just these four words. They will get married in secret and immediately take a leave from work and run off to the country. Yes, after the defense her life will finally begin! Everything before was just a prologue, an overture. First, she thought: "I will graduate from high school and start living for real"; then: "I will go to college, and..."

And later: "I have to graduate from college, and then..."

Now there is no more "then"! She promised herself to leave the race after her thesis defense. And what she promised herself is carved in stone.

Now it all hangs on the thesis. Or, rather, on the condition of Sidorina. If Sidorina lives, the PhD is a certainty. Again, that "if"! Out of the six patients, three were alive. Fifty percent. One more successful surgery... "If" was such a slippery word.

"Irina Yakovlevna, it's for you!"

"Yes, speaking. Hello, Natalia Nikolayevna. I see... I see... Too bad. How is Mokeyeva? What?! Yttrium was injected on the 16th, right? Today is the 30th. Calm down, Natalia Nikolayevna, don't... let's not make any hasty conclusions. Give it a few more days."

"Irina Yakovlevna, a minute?"

"What's wrong?"

"Nothing, Irina".

"You are crazy. People talk about us as it is."

"They are jealous."

"Of whom?"

"You, of course."

"Aren't you a bit arrogant, mister?"

"Irina... Irinochka!"

"What's up with you today?"

"I'm in a good mood."

"You always are. I'm feeling..."

"Uneasy?"

"Yes."

"Out with it."

"Mokeyeva is going the same way as the first three."

"Already?.."

"Not yet, but the signs are there."

"Uh-oh."

"In half an hour... thirty-five minutes... I'll have Sidorina on the operation table. I don't know why, but I feel something for her... I can't let her... You understand?"

"A doctor can't afford to have feelings. It's not going to be long, now. Your thesis subject is fascinating. It's a new treatment that has hardly been used in this country before. The preliminary tests showed that yttrium was effective. The brain tumors disappeared. You have a bright future. Bukhtin himself will accept you. And because of your feelings... I'm sorry, but it is silly. We are not a community clinic. We are a medical research facility. We do research! We are interested in the disease more than in the patient. If the price of saving hundreds is sacrificing one, or six, or a dozen, so be it! We have to take risks for this noble goal. Do not ruin your future. She is not a person, not a Maria Sidorina, but a subject of..."

"It's Tatiana."

"Ok, Tatiana. A test subject."

"That is true, but..."

"No buts! No questioning yourself! Only the cold mind of a talented doctor!"

He is right. He is right. Irina Yakovlevna hurries down the endless corridor. He is right. Everything hangs on her thesis defense. And that is the only subject she can defend. She cannot waste years and start over because of some fleeting emotion, some silly compassion. How stupid. What kind of doctor would she be? A weakling! A freshman who faints at the sight of a cadaver.

She peeks into the doctors' mess.

"Halochka, I'll be in surgery."

"Who is operating on Sidorina?"

"Doctor Karpinsky."

Her heels drum a staccato on the stairs again. This time the sound is hard. Irina Yakovlevna goes one floor down and enters a hallway. Sidorina is being rolled on a gurney. The patient's gaze is on the ceiling, indifferent. In Sidorina's eye there is no hint of excruciating pain or fear.

Irina, as usual, intends to remain silent and only smile encouragingly. Instead, she asks: "How's the mood today?"

She thinks she sees a shadow of a bitter, even sarcastic, smile on Sidorina's face. Indeed, the question is strange, even ridiculous. Irina blushes slightly.

What is wrong with her? Why is she so anxious? Stupid female intuition! Her heart races. She must get a hold on herself. Everything is going according to the plan. Everything is fine! The efficiency of yttrium will be proven. It will! Even if Sidorina... Well, it is necessary for science.

"Tatiana Sergeyevna, everything will be okay."

She gives the patient one more encouraging glance and is about to hurry into the operating room, but something makes her hesitate. It is then that Sidorina says quietly and with a child's faith: 'I trust you, doctor."

"*I trust you, doctor*," Irina hears as if from a distance. "*I trust you, doctor.*" The words grow bigger and fill the corridor. *I trust you, doctor... I trust you!.. Doctor!*

Irina leans close to Sidorina and whispers: "Refuse the surgery."

Sidorina refused.

"Sorry, Man, Duty Calls!"

The lobby of Ostankino TV studio was crowded. People sat on benches, stood by the cigarette vending machines and at the pass office window.

He weaved his way among the people, careful not to shove anyone, and apologized if someone jostled him.

A short, wrinkled, snub-nosed guard, his head held proudly up, took his time to study the pass.

"Ilya Anatolyevich Krupitsky. Please, go ahead."

He approached Building 4. It was almost noon. He ascended the stairs, saying a polite hello to everyone he met. People ran past him up and down the steps.

"Hey, man! How's it going?"

He stopped.

"I have..."

"Sorry, gotta run. I'll see you later."

He stood for a time and then went on.

"Hey, Ilya! It's been ages! How have you been?"

"Not good."

"What's up? Have they taken you off air? They'll regret that. Cheer up. Call me later!"

He walked the long corridor.

"*All children play outside. All children fall and come home scratched and bruised... How she wept when she broke her leg!.. She enjoyed watching parakeets peck at seeds...*"

"Hello! Listen, Krupitsky, did you make *Spring Walks the Streets*?"

"No."

"Who, then?"

"I don't know."

"...She liked wearing a cast. She had lots of time to draw and she didn't have to brush her hair. She didn't like brushing her hair. She would ask, 'Papa, tell me a story'".

"Why the long face, pal? Is something wrong?"

"Oh, hi. A great tragedy."

"What's up?"

Someone yelled from a distant door: "Yevgeny, we are about to start!"

"Coming! Sorry, pal, gotta run!"

"There you go," the doctor had said. "She'll be running soon." Running... What could he have done differently? What?

"Papa, my leg hurts." "It's okay, baby. It'll get better soon."

"Cheers, Ilya. Have you seen Sasha?"

"No."

"I recommend hospitalization. The bone has fused wrong. It can only be fixed in-patient."

"Papa, tell me a story." "Sleep, child."

"Ilya! Wait up! I heard something happened. What is going on?"

"Something bad happened. You see, my daughter..."

"What's wrong with her? Do you need anything? I can help. What's the problem?"

A shout: "Everyone to the planning meeting! Move!"

"Where?"

"Screening room? Now! It's urgent."

"Urgent? Interesting... Are you coming?"

"No."

"I think I'll go check it out. See ya."

"Papa, hey, Papa, how do I draw clouds on white paper? They are white!" "If they're thunderclouds, they are gray." "What if they're not?" "Then color the sky blue and leave white spaces for clouds."

"What's wrong, doctor?" "I called you, because... You see... There is a tumor at the site of the bone fusion. It is not malignant, but..."

She spent more and more time looking out of the window. Especially when it rained.

The editors' room was empty. So was the directors'. The corridor was full of slender female assistants in skinny jeans and their young pimply male counterparts carrying some sort of paper forms.

"The biopsy has confirmed sarcoma. Let's put our hopes in Professor Dovyalov."

"Papa, please, take me home!" "Have they been treating you badly here?" "No. I even made some friends. But I still want to go home!"

"...I won't." "You have to eat. You need your strength." "I don't want to." "Nobody is going to reheat the food for you." "I don't want it anyway." "You will eat!" "I won't!" "I said you will!" "No!" "Enough! I'm tired of you being cranky!"

"Once there lived a Prince. He was ugly, but very smart. One day..."

He was standing at the door of the screening room when a wave of people poured out.

"Hi Ilya!"

"Hello!"

"Good afternoon!"

"Hello, Ilya Anatolyevich!"

"Greetings, man!"

He would turn to respond, but someone else was already asking: "How's life, Ilya?"

He wanted to tell that person how life was, but someone else was asking: "What's new?" From every direction he was overwhelmed by "What's up?", "How are you?", "How's it going?"... He kept turning to respond, but could not pinpoint the one who asked.

"Papa, it hurts. Tell them not to touch me. Tell them to leave it alone. I don't want to. Tell them, Papa..." "Shh, babygirl, shhh, calm down, you have to be quiet. Hold on, baby, the doctor will be here soon..." "I don't want the doctor. I want to go home! I don't like it here, it hurts, Papa, dear Papa, take me away, take me home, please..."

"Something bad happened! Listen! My daughter... Wait! Wait up! Listen to me! My baby girl... she..."

He stood, silent. The screening room was empty but for the janitor who was picking up papers and candy wrappers.

"Aunt Asya!"

"What is it, son?"

"My daughter died today."

"Your daughter?"

"Yes."

"She died? Why are you even here?"

"I couldn't stay home... I don't know how I got here..."

"Was she ill?"

"She was."

"How old?"

"Just turned eight."

"Dear Lord! Well, can't do anything about it now, can you?.. You know what? Write a letter to the financial aid office for some money."

"Come on, Aunt Asya, what for?"

"What for? Do you know how expensive funerals are? You have to pay for the plot, for the marker, for the engraving, and for the music... You poor thing!.. Nothing else you can do. Go ahead, write. I buried my old man a bit ago, I know. Write like this: *To the Financial Aid office from so-and-so, an employee of the studio. Due to the tragic untimely loss of my young daughter* — put her name there — *I am requesting monetary assistance in the amount of...* — put the amount there, then date and sign. There. Take it to them. They have to help. Now, go home. You should be home."

"Thank you, Aunt Asya."

"Go, honey, go. Go home."

He stuck the letter in his pocket and walked to the door.

"Hey, man! How's it going?"

"It's going."

"Right on! See ya."

Concerto
for a Choir and Phonograph

W ell, it all happened back in the Soviet days. Right before Christmas, the performers arrived. Ours is a small village, but we do have an inn — one story and a snack bar. The bar sometimes has beer. But that's not important now. Just figured I'd mention, in case.

The actors were lodged in the inn. The eight men had a room for eight, and so did the women — for the women-folk. How do I know? Well, Marusya runs the bar. She's a feisty wench, that one… But that's not important now. Just figured I'd mention.

We had known about them coming, because as soon as the bus showed up on the highway, the kids came shouting all over the village: "The performers are here!" So, the women and girls, who were not working, ran to the club for the tickets. There was a poster already out about a pop-music concert. By the ticket booth stood Valentina, the club director; she had been married to Vaska Simeonov, and when Vaska went back to drinking, she hooked up with Mishka Temnov, and when she and Mishka fell out, she got this job at the club. But that's not important now. Just figured I'd mention.

Well, the concert was sold out just like that. We were waiting for the evening, since that's when it was to start.

Everyone got dressed up. As for me, I dug out my tie, the glittery one, that I had bought thirty years before that from a Gypsy woman in Tula. Had to haggle for it, too! She was selling makeup for wenches, but I didn't buy any. My woman had no business painting her face.

The women showed up at the concert in full war paint, in wigs, or shawls, or fluffy woolen hats. The men were in ski jackets over colorful shirts with words on them, or even leather vests. Some guys wore buzz cuts, some had shaved heads, some had long hair — from behind you couldn't even tell if it was a gal or a guy. The only difference was, gals squealed.

Well, everyone took a good look at one another and had enough time to posture before the lights went out. We clapped, for sure. The curtain was pulled apart. It did get stuck for a bit in the middle. But Valentina rose from the first row, climbed up on the stage, and gave it a mighty tug. The curtain went right into place. We clapped again. Valentina bowed like an actress and sat back down.

Then, a performer came onto the stage. Holy smokes! Heels four fingers high, black patent shoes, red socks... White pants that you could see through where there was no lining. His shirt was yellow, with lace, the bowtie was green with white polka dots, and his jacket — velvet purple. He was a redhead, with long sideburns. A real African parrot, I tell you what. A beauty! A color TV! Soon as he showed up, the gals almost jumped out of their dresses to see him better. In front of me Zinka Goncharova breathed: "Whoa, girls!..." — and plopped back down. I felt kinda bad for her. Her boyfriend Mitka Kubarev is nothing to look at — pale, small, a carrot of a guy. But that's not important now. Just figured I'd mention, in case someone's in the market.

The performer, sure thing, said hello into the mike and started greeting us all on behalf of the performers, his town, and himself. Then he congratulated us on some job well done, milk yields and harvests. And all that rhymed. Now tell me, how could he make it all up in rhymes? Right... Then he called the musicians onto the stage. Four guys came out, dressed all the same, no ties, shirts unbuttoned, but the belts were nice. They picked up their guitars, flipped some switches, and their machines made such an awful howl! Then something screeched, crackled, gargled, jerked... and the lights went out. They must have shortened something there. Or the fuses blew, or some such. But that's when the most interesting part began.

Naturally, the folks made all kinds of commotion — whistled, stomped their feet; someone made a loud kissing noise and everyone else roared with laughter.

Mr. Bowtie was saying it was okay and we could still have fun. He said something else, but it was hard to hear him without the mike. So he asked loudly if there was an electrician in the audience. Valentina jumped up and was rushing about, looking, but where was an electrician when you needed one? And time was passing. The folks were grumbling. The performers were restless. Might be they had the next concert they had to get to. What to do? Then Bowtie said — don't worry, the show will go on. While the search for an electrician continued, the performers who did not need light or music or the mike would provide entertainment. No time would be wasted! So, everyone got quiet, and someone began reciting poems, a male voice.

One poem. We clapped. Another. And another. We got bored of clapping. But the man kept going. Well, great, we thought, he wasn't gonna shut up until an electrician was found. However, the man got tired also. "I'm done!" he said and left. Then someone else came on the stage and sang in a female voice, with no music. Just like the village wenches at a get-together, but alone. She sang one song. We were thinking, what's next? And she also said "I'm done!" We, naturally, asked her for more. And she said that she refused to sing more without the band. Shame! Mayhaps she was even pretty, a sight for sore eyes — if we had light, that was. On the other hand, what if she was an ugly witch? Nah, better we didn't have light. Anyway, I'm babbling.

So, it was still dark. Bowtie came back and said: "Now, you will see some magic tricks!" The folks started grumbling what kind of tricks, in the dark? In the dark anyone could do magic, better than a magician could in the light!

Then, Valentina appeared with a fancy candle holder full of candles. Leftovers from the drama club, she said. Here you go, dear performers, perform away.

Everyone, naturally, rejoiced and applauded Valentina. Now we could watch magic tricks.

Now, Bowtie was back and said that the magician always performed to music and now was not an exception and he was asking if we had someone who played accordion, or at least an accordion to play. We got quiet and thinking-like. It was freezing outside, naturally. It was warm inside. Someone would still go, if there was an accordion to be had. Kolka used to have one, but it got ripped to shreds at a wedding where Kolka was stupid enough to ogle the bride. Well, to be fair, she ogled him right back. Mayhaps it was serious, but what did the poor accordion do? Nobody else had an accordion. I had an old one in the attic, but all the buttons were gone.

Well, we were just sitting there. Then Valentina popped up again and ran backstage. In a minute, she returned with a dusty phonograph. Go figure! I had forgotten what one of those things looked like! An antique. A fossil.

Valentina opened the lid and said that she borrowed the phonograph also from the drama club, and it was a stage prop.

Alright, we had the phonograph, and it even had a needle, but there was only one record. Valentina asked the performers not to take offense — the record was part of a play and it was an aria. Well, not like they had a choice, had they. Bowtie said, whatever, and announced the magician. The magician did his tricks and the record played, as if it knew: "*A hundred tricks, and everything will be the way I want.*"

He was done, and some dancers danced the hopak to the same music! "I will fear no-one!" — and they did the hopak! Well, we weren't born in a barn, either. Civilized like all get out!

Then nobody showed up for a while. Then Bowtie appeared and again announced the same singer, sarcastic-like. She took her time, that one. Figured she didn't want to sing, but Bowtie made her. Then she came out and said she was going to sing the aria on the record, with the record. A duet! So she did. We listened and clapped. Someone even sang along quietly. By the end of the song, the phonograph started hissing — the needle got all worn down.

Bowtie said, too bad the needle got worn down, since there were two more numbers to go.

Go ahead, we yelled, we can sing no worse than the record! We had memorized the aria by then, see.

Here came the juggler. We started clapping the rhythm and at first sang all out of order. Then we got better. It was even pretty, like on the radio. The juggler was throwing his rings and balls, and we sang. Dunno about the performers, but we liked our singing. When we got done, we even clapped.

Then Bowtie said: now, sing one more time and we'll be saying our goodbyes. The director, he said, came up with this interesting finale.

We, of course, sang. Why not? "And I give in, I give in to everyone, in everything..." And the performers came out to bow. Bowtie said some words, the performers raised their linked hands and hurried off.

Us folks, we stayed a long time. Nobody wanted to leave. Nobody even got out of their seats.

I said: "One more time, guys?" They laughed at first and then started singing for real. Very nicely, too. With different voices. And then, before the song was over, the lights came back on. The electrician had showed up and changed the fuse. As soon as the lights came on, the song sort of faded. Kinda like it wasn't needed, what with the lights on.

Someone yelled: "Turn it off! We're singing here!" Valentina went and turned the lights off. And we picked the song back up.

We mostly sang old songs, almost forgotten, what we had heard from the old women as little kids. It was nice. Intimate. That was a real concert we put up for ourselves. The performers couldn't hold a candle to us — so to speak.

We sang until the candles burned out.

A Picture Book

He was about forty; I, twelve years younger. He seemed a bit strange: a blatantly old-fashioned bow tie with drooping ends, a brown cane with a white metal knob, and a pince-nez were the things that you noticed first upon meeting him. He had an odd way of speaking, too: "I serve in such-and-such office". Or, "I go to serve at such-and-such place." Or: "Yes-tereve, the theater put on such-and-such performance." At the same time, he loved the ultra-modern vocabulary of the articles on education, psychology, sociology, medicine, philosophy, and avant-garde art. Sometimes he would let his sparse gray mustaches grow out for a couple of weeks and then suddenly shave them off. He had a slight lisp and spoke quietly, although with confidence. Everything he said sounded convincing.

His small room was also strange, with its old rickety furniture, drab, stained wallpaper, and a wooden bed that was never made. Nothing sat on top of the cheap unpolished desk, except a rather thick layer of dust.

Still, I enjoyed visiting him. I would enter without a word and sit on a high-backed chair, writing, reading, or just staring at the wall…

One evening, I went to see him, as I often did, without notice. Nobody answered the doorbell. I pushed the door — it was unlocked — and walked into the narrow dark hallway. The silence was normal, but I still felt anxious. I walked into the room.

The furniture had been randomly moved. I bumped into the desk, walked around it and saw my host. He lay on the floor under the window, awkwardly leaning on the radiator. His eyes were open, his gaze was empty and distant. In his left hand (he was not left-handed) he held a kitchen knife and was trying to slice through the inside of his elbow with its dull edge.

I ran up, snatched away the knife, tossed it aside, and did my best to rouse him: I shook him, slapped his face, shouted, and tried to get him up on his feet. Eventually, his eyelashes fluttered; he closed his eyes; the tension went out of his body and it became limp and heavy. I dragged him to the bed and he fell onto it, exhausted.

I should have called the doctor, but my friend had no phone. I hadn't brought mine, and the closest public phone was on the other side of the street. With no idea what to do I helplessly shuffled my feet at his bedside. He opened his eyes.

"Are you feeling better?" I asked. "Shall I call the doctor?"

"No. I'm okay. Go home."

"I can't leave you alone!"

"Go. I'll be fine."

He said that last in such a strong voice that I believed it was alright to leave him.

On my way home, I tried to guess what his ailment was. I was certain it was life-threatening. But how could I help? I spent the night thinking.

The next day I saw him at work. I awkwardly said hello, received an indifferent response, and we parted ways. I tried to avoid looking at him. He averted his eyes also.

A week passed.

Everything is eventually forgotten. Our relationship went back to normal. Yet, I did not return to his place.

One day he came to me and asked me to visit that night. I declined at first, but he was so insistent that I had to say yes.

His room looked the same. I sat on the chair. He seemed like he was about to tell me something personal and important.

"I'm not sure..." he began, carefully choosing his words. "How to say that... But you saw some of it, so it should be easier to understand..."

He went to his bed and brought from under the pillow a large book in a bright mosaic cover.

"Here".

I reached out to take it, but he did not let me.

"Not yet. Listen to me first."

He put the book aside and, losing his train of thought here and there, began telling his improbable story.

I could not concentrate on it at first and did not understand much for that reason.

Excited, he talked about choosing a world, one of four, and that the things around us could think... I tried to interject, but he insisted that some people can reach the Higher World, the Real one, while others existed in the other three; that those three were only reflections of the High World, fantasy reflections, secondary, whatever you want to call them, but not Real; that we had the freedom to choose what world to live in, but this freedom was limited, because we were surrounded by four virtual walls, of which only one led to the Real World, and the odds of choosing correctly were one to three; that three quarters of people lived in the wrong world, including himself; that in his world inanimate things ruled, had a mind, reigned over humans, could move and communicate with one another, controlled a human's life and played with it, eventually destroying the human... His next words were complete nonsense. In a whisper, breathless, he told me that the things conspired to murder him with his own hands. He said that on the day I found him, he had sat at the table, cutting bologna for a sandwich. Suddenly, an unknown force pulled the chair from under him. He fell. At the same moment, the table kicked him hard towards the window and trapped him next to the radiator. Then something, against his will, made him draw the blade on his arm several times: that's what I saw when I had walked in on him that night.

He finished talking. His hands shook. His lips were pale and thin.

I could not utter a word. It was hard to find words. I was also scared. In front of me sat a crazy man, I had no doubt about that.

"You don't believe me," he said with unexpected calm. "Shame. Now, look at the book one more time. It's all there."

29

He handed me the book. I did not want to upset a sick man, so I took it and opened it. There were only four pages. It reminded me of a children's pop-up book with silly poorly drawn illustrations.

"Do you see now?" he asked quietly.

"Yes, you are right, of course," I said, putting the book aside and standing up to leave.

"You still don't believe me."

"I'm sorry, I have to go," I said awkwardly. "It's late."

I put my coat on and walked out into the street.

I had nightmares that night. Tables and chairs flew. The bed laughed maniacally. I sat in a big cookpot that screeched along the pavement at insane speed. Several times I woke and turned over, forcing my eyes open and saying: "It is only a dream!" — but as soon as my eyes closed, the nightmare returned, oppressive and crushing. I got up before dawn, dressed and went outside. The snowstorm howled. The wind pierced me through. I shrank, pulled my head into the narrow collar of my coat and set off wandering the streets; I had to recover, to walk off the nightmare.

There was not a soul in sight. It was dark. Sharp, hard snow hit me in the face. At times, I felt as if I was still dreaming.

I don't know how I ended up at his place. I went up the stairs. I opened the door — it wasn't locked, again. I entered and switched on the light.

Panic and horror seized me. My legs went limp. My tongue stuck to the roof of my mouth. My God, what a sight!

He lay on the bed, dressed in his new suit. His head was tilted back. The veins of his left arm were cut open and blood trickled to the floor. With the same kitchen knife in his right hand, he convulsively sliced through his already gaping throat. Thick dark blood gushed out and onto his white starched shirt and the white sheet. I heard gurgling coming from his throat, but it was obviously too late.

Horrified, I ran outside and pounded on a neighbor's door, yelling for help. Someone called the ambulance and the police.

A week went by. I felt restless and guilty—I had not attended his funeral or visited his grave after.

"I should go to the cemetery," I decided.

First, though, I wanted to visit his place.

Dust covered everything. The room was quiet and empty. His relatives had taken away his clothes, shoes, linens, and other things. In the room stood two lonely old chairs, a table, a heavy dark cupboard, and the wooden bed with a striped mattress; on the mattress sat the book. I wiped the dust off with my sleeve and opened it. Instead of the silly illustrations, on each of the four pages was the grinning face of the deceased. It was a caricature. He wore his new suit, his bow tie, and his pince-nez. His sparse hair barely covered his balding forehead. He was grinning, but the look in his eyes was mean.

I thought I was hallucinating. Then, the book began to grow. It surrounded me on all four sides. I found myself in a tiny cell. From the four walls, four faces stared at me. I tried to break through, but the pages were rock solid. The cell began to rotate. Faster, faster, faster! Suddenly, it stopped. For several seconds, I dumbly stared at the walls and could not control either my thoughts or my body. I felt terrified. Like a crazed animal, I threw myself at one of the page-walls seeking to either break through or kill myself.

A wide, snow-covered road leads into the distance. I walk, leaning forward into the piercing wind. With both hands, I hug to myself a picture book. My eyes are wide open.

Slowly,
a table
flies by.

Sack Race

The coach is talking to the athlete.

"You have to, get it? Ever heard the word 'must'?"

"That's not my area," the athlete argues. "I am a sprinter, and that's a marathon."

"Well, you can, of course, say no. Like Hurevich did. Did you know him?"

"Did I know him? I still know him."

"So, you did."

"What's wrong? Has something happened to him?" the athlete asks, concerned.

"Nah, he's fine. He refused to run the marathon. Nothing wrong with him, he just isn't getting paid."

The athlete paled.

"Alright, I'll run," he conceded.

The team had gathered. Before the start, everyone was issued a sack.

"What's that for? To carry the snacks in?"

"To carry you. Get in. It's a sack marathon. Didn't you know?"

"A sack marathon? What does that mean? Why? I don't..."

...But he ran. Or, rather, hopped.

Alongside him hopped good, solid men, capable athletes.

"What kind of marathon is this? Who had the brilliant idea?" the athlete, a champion sprinter, resented. "This sack race is stupid!"

"Stupid!" someone agreed.

The fellow hoppers nodded their heads and grumbled.

"We have better things to do!"

"Whoever came up with this can go hop himself!"

"Right! Why do they make us do it?"

"Enough! Drop the sacks and let's go home!" the racers shouted, one hand in the air, while the other held up the sack.

"Well, are we done, then?" the athlete asked carefully.

"Yeah!" the one next to him agreed. "You first!"

"Why me?"

"Well, who else?"

"You."

"No way, dude. I'm not dumb. I'll drop mine and the rest of you won't. Everyone will look like everyone else, and I'm going to be naked? Nope. I'll drop mine when you guys drop yours."

"Then you take it off", the athlete said to another man.

"Why?" the other one said warily. "I'm fine in the sack. It's like a free uniform. I'm warm and not bothered by flies."

"I saw you protesting the loudest!"

"Me?! I'm like the other guys. They shouted, and so did I. I'm always with the other guys!" he hopped ahead with enthusiasm, trying to distance himself from our hero.

"Listen," the athlete asked the runner in spectacles. "You look like a smart person and should understand that running in a sack is ridiculous."

"I know that."

'Why won't you drop it?"

"I believe your question is a trick question, to some extent, and I could leave it unanswered. But I will answer it. Yes, running in a sack is awkward. At first. If you haven't done it before. Yes, it is absurd. Maybe even idiotic. But listen, if I take the sack off, I'll be ahead of everyone else. I'll take the lead! This can be misconstrued. And who am I by myself, without the team? Without any roots, so to speak? A tumbleweed! Besides, many have tried running without sacks. Where are they now? Running in sacks is for us! It's familiar, it's what we do. We are proud of it! We are all in a sack together, hopping ahead to victory, to the bright light of the finish!"

The smart guy pulled his sack up to his chin and hopped away.

"How about you, man?" the athlete asked a hulk of a guy with a shaved head. "How's your run?"

"It's bullcrap!"

"Really?" The champion seemed to have found a fellow rebel. "Why's that?"

"What kind of competition is this? In sacks! The last time, we played soccer, and they tied our feet together with a rope and glued our arms to our heads. That was a real game! And the winners got a case of vodka! This one... No fun at all. Well, they do say they'll be a bottle of booze at the finish line. That's why I'm running."

Ahead was a huge muddy puddle. There was no way to go around it, so the crowd ran straight into the mud.

"That's really not bad at all!" rejoiced the first one to come out on the other side, the leader. "I'm actually starting to like it. Hardship builds character!"

Leaving muddy footprints, hopping, the sack team ran on.

"Ah, screw it!" the athlete thought. "I'll get to the finish line and leave sports for good!"

...He had no idea that the sack race had no end.

A New Carnival Ride

"**A** new original ride! You won't regret it! Only a coin, and any one of you, regardless of your color or weight, can become a blue air balloon and fly wherever you want! Only a coin! An all new ride!"

A crowd gathered around the barker. Whoa! Fly wherever you want?! Isn't that everyone's lifelong dream?

Someone in the crowd remembered that this ride was a great success a year before. Many brave people dared to fulfill their dream. Strangely, though, none of them came back. Why was that? Did they end up in a place so nice that they didn't want to return, or... oh the horror... were they dead?

"Did they at least write?"

"A few excited letters at first, then nothing."

"Maybe they realized they made a mistake and are too embarrassed to admit it?"

"Or they are so happy that they don't want to share with us!"

"Why wouldn't they?"

"I think I have a coin to spare..."

Getting to the ticket booth was not easy — many wanted to try the ride. The stronger ones broke through, dropped a coin in the machine, and the booth doors opened for them. A human walked in, and after a minute, a blue balloon appeared from an opening at the top.

One by one the balloons rose high into the sky. They were very proud of themselves, puffed up and their wrinkles smoothed out. They watched those who remained on the ground condescendingly, like a human watches earthworms.

One balloon rose to the top of the tallest tree.

"Wow!" he thought. "It's beautiful! I can see far all around. I like it here. I don't know what comes next. I think I'll stay here."

It hooked onto a tree branch.

"Stupid", the others thought. "He does not dream big. We are not going to stop! Onward and skyward!"

They floated on. They stopped looking down and so did not see some boys using their slingshots to shoot down the balloon that was stuck in the tree. They could not see it. But they did hear an odd sound, like a balloon popping.

They flew on. Now they were nearing the top of the tallest TV tower in town. One balloon sat on the point of the antenna.

"My goodness, how wonderful!" he marveled. "I feel like a bird! I want to build a nest up here, on this antenna, at the top of happiness. And the added bonus is I'm going to be the first to watch new TV programs!"

This balloon could not know that it would cause TV interference; a worker would climb the tower and, cursing profusely, reach the balloon, let the air out of it, and toss it into the dumpster.

The rest of the balloons kept rising. They flew towards the sun. There were so many of them that they formed a cloud, a blue cloud that covered the sun.

The people on the ground rejoiced when they saw a cloud, even a blue one. There had been no rain for a long time. The earth dried up and cracked, exhausted from the heat. Finally, there was a cloud. But what if the wind blew it away? What if it did not produce rain?

The people brought out a cannon, a special cannon that shoots into a cloud to make it rain. There was a boom and it started to rain. It was real rain. But it was strange — it tasted salty, like tears.

A Wagon

A wagon enters the road. It is pulled by a hulk of a guy with a face of a permanently surprised child. In the wagon sits a small arrogant person with a face of a cranky old man. The little man holds a whip which he repeatedly uses on the hulk.

"Whoa! Whoa!"

"See, I'm tired," retorts the hulk, not unkindly. "Come on. I have been pulling you forever. Give me a break."

"Whoa! Whoa!"

"Dang you!" the hulk stops. "Leave me alone! That's it. I'm not going any further."

"Whoa! Whoa!"

"Nope, I'm done. Where did you come from, anyway? Where? Showed up just like that. I never even seen you before. Just shows up and says — come here, I'll tell you somethin. So I went."

"Whoa! Whoa!"

"Whoa you! I don't even know who you are. Who are you, eh? Eh? Stand here, he says. Pick up the shafts, he says, and pull. So, I pulled. Who he is, I don't even know."

"Whoa! Whoa!"

"Go to... Whoa yourself! Come try pulling it, and I'll watch."

"Whoa! Whoa!"

"Hell, that's enough! Get down from there right now! I said I won't go and I won't. For God's sake, leave me be! What did I do to deserve it? Pull, he says. And I... For real!"

"Whoa! Whoa!"

"Shut up! And get down off there! I said get down! Or I'll throw you off. See if I don't!"

"Whoa! Whoa!"

"Oh, that's how it's gonna be? Alright. You asked for it, you little devil. Just wait..."

The hulk approaches the little man, grabs him by the scruff of the neck, and tosses him out of the wagon. The little guy flips head over heels and lands on a rock at the shoulder of the road. It obviously hurts. He screams his head off for everyone to hear.

"Much better," says the hulk and sits down on the edge of the wagon to rest. "I will not pull you. No sir! Pull, he says. I'm such a fool... Cry me a river! It won't do you any good. I don't even know who he is. Who, from where? What does he want? Just won't leave me be. Take the shafts, he says... And I don't even know him!"

The little guy lies in the dirt, his arms and legs spread wide, sobbing.

"Why are you crying? Stop it! Are you hurt? Well, did you think it was easy for me to drag you around in this rattletrap? Right!"

The little guy throws a tantrum, drumming his heels on the ground.

"There, there," the hulk gets up, worried, and goes to the little guy. "Goodness. Come on, stop it. Stop it, I said! I don't even know where he came from, so pitiful... There, don't cry, you hear? Don't cry. How he wails, poor thing. Why did I listen? Pull, he says. Alright, alright, that's enough. Well? Goodness, look at him go. Stop wailing, you little devil! What do you want? Want a lollipop? No? What, then? Want me to dance?"

The little guy nods, still sobbing.

"Here, watch," the hulk says and starts stomping his feet and clapping his hands, raising clouds of dust.

The little guy stops crying and watches the hulk kneading the dirt with his feet and his arms cutting the air like blades of a windmill.

The hulk stops, panting and wiping off sweat.

"Phew... It's hard to do... without music... Happy now?"

In response, the little guy lets out a new wail. Bitter tears again run down the beaten paths of his wrinkled face.

"Holy geez!" the hulk swears. "Why did I get into this? The devil must have confounded me! What the hell else do you want from me? Want me to sing? There! Baa-baa black sheep, have you any wool? Yes sir, yes sir, three bags full!"

The little guy cries.

"How about a cartwheel?"

The hulk cartwheels.

"Lord, what more?!"

The little guy, still crying, points at the wagon.

"Where did you come from? Where do you want me to take you? Pick up the shafts, he says, and pull..."

The hulk picks up the little guy, carefully dusts him off, wipes his nose, and puts him in the wagon. The little guy immediately stops crying and snatches up the whip.

"Whoa! Whoa!"

"I'm working on it!" The hulk picks up the shafts, leans forward, and the wagon starts moving with a squeal. "Come here, he says, I'll tell you something... And just like that, I'm harnessed up... Little devil!"

"Whoa! Whoa!" the little guy yells joyfully and waves the whip.

The hulk pulls the wagon.

"I'm not going to pull you," he grumbles. "And he says, yes, you are... I ain't, no, sir!.."

He walks away, pulling the wagon.

House of Mirrors

A house of mirrors. Distorted mirrors on the walls. Normal ordinary people walk inside, and in the mirrors appear fat dwarves on stunted legs or thin people, stretched like noodles, or squashed twins. People laugh at themselves in the mirrors. It is a place to laugh.

A short, hunchbacked, ugly man entered. He looked at himself in the mirror and saw a slim, handsome man. The hunchback took a mirror off the wall and blocked the exit door with it.

"Look, look at me! Haha, check you out!.."

"That's ridiculous! Hey, look at this one, he's hilarious!"

"Who?"

"That hunchback! Haha!"

"Shush! He's like that for real."

"Nah, he's fine, look..."

"That's his reflection."

"Noooo!" the hunchback screamed. "All of us are real in the mirrors! Here, out of the mirrors, we are all filthy beasts! Beasts!... Bring me a chair!"

Someone obligingly set a chair in the middle of the room.

"Listen to my command!" he screamed, spitting. "Around me... march!"

People, as if hypnotized, started walking single-file around the hunchback.

"Move it, move it!" the ugly man urged them on, lounging in the chair with his legs spread wide.

And people walked faster. Normal, regular people obeyed the hunchback's order without a word. The mirrors reflected funny ugly little folks running around a noble handsome man on a throne.

"Hey!" one of the walkers whispered to the one in front of him. "What the hell is that? Why are we obeying him like puppets? He's no better than us!"

"He's better in the mirror."

"In the mirror, not in real life!"

"I'm confused. I don't know what's real and what's the reflection. Maybe it's the other way 'round."

"Nonsense! Miss," he turned to the girl behind him, "you do see that we are being ordered around by a filthy hunchback..."

"Filthy hunchback? But you are mistaken! He is wonderful! He is better than a thousand the likes of you! He is my idol!"

And she, eager to obey and overwhelmed with adoration, pumped her legs even faster.

"Listen!.. I..."

"Be quiet!" he was admonished from every side. "Don't interfere with us doing what we are told. We are all in it together now, like a well-oiled machine. This is amazing! He unified us! He showed us the way! He... He... He... The great one! The mighty one! The most slender one! The most handsome! The mostest!"

And they proceeded to obey the hunchback's commands with even greater enthusiasm, ecstatic.

"No way," thought the doubting one. "I have to get out of here, away from these distorted mirrors and distorted people. Where is the exit? I think it was over there..."

But there is no exit over there. There is another mirror. It reflects a funny ugly man looking for a way out.

This is a House of Mirrors.

The Specter

*"A specter is haunting Europe —
the specter of Communism."*

The Communist Manifesto

I am a simple man; they call me, *intelligentsia*. Naturally, I wear spectacles, and all that. Your typical "disposable" person. My brow is wrinkled by the eternal questions: "What to do?", "Who is to blame?", and "To leave or not to leave?" While I'm scrunching my brow, the next generation, represented by my third-grader son, drills monotonously:

"A specter is haunting Europe... A specter is haunting Europe... A specter is haunting..."

"I wish it were just Europe," I think to myself. "It is haunting Asia, Africa, and America too. Why leave, then? It will catch up with me anywhere..."

"Papa, do you believe in specters?" my son asks.

I immediately realize that too much hangs on my answer. I will never forget Brecht's *Spy* and the parents that were afraid of being reported to the authorities by their own son. I also remember the "heroic deed" of Pavlik Morozov who ratted his Papa out to Cheka and became a shining example to several generations of the Soviet Young Pioneers... What if my son decides to be a national hero?! I can already hear him telling the teacher: "My Papa does not believe in specters!" The teacher quotes him at the parent-teacher conference in the presence of a person in plain civilian clothes. And then...

"I do! I do believe in specters!" I shout.

It's a trap.

"Pop, what is a specter?"

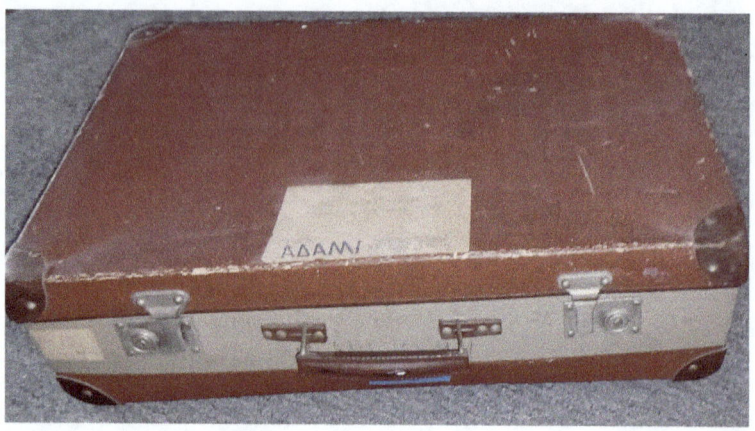

From the frying pan into the fire... I pace the room, rubbing my sweating bald head.

"A specter is... it is..." I don't know what to say and I stall for time. The ghost of Hamlet's father invades my thoughts. Hamlet's *dead* father!

"I think, Pop, it's someone who died and then his ghost started showing up. Right? He's not here anymore, but he still kinda is. Right, Pop? Like a vampire. What is a vampire?"

I jump to the phone and smother it with a pillow. Then I turn up both the radio and the TV. I run water in the bathtub. I shut the doors and windows. I make sure not a single specter or vampire hears my son's questions. He, however, continues in a ringing voice:

"A vampire is someone who died and then became alive again and drinks blood from people, right?"

That's pure provocation! He demands affirmation from me!

"What sort of nonsense is that?" I shout intentionally loudly, warily looking over my shoulder. "What does it have to do with vampires? It's a completely different matter! It's the brightest... the most... for all people... It's about..." I switch to whisper. "If you don't want me to be banished from the Party and lose my job, and all of us to... I have no idea, but nothing good... stop it now! And don't even think about repeating all this at school!"

"I'm not stupid," he looks at me with such understanding that I immediately relax.

My son goes into the bathroom and shuts off the water. He takes the pillow off the phone. He turns off the radio that is broadcasting the nation's great achievements. He turns off the TV that shows the nation marching towards the bright communist future. Then he sits down and opens the book again.

He is so much like me, this boy of mine! His brow wrinkles like mine. He thinks about the same things. Just like his father. He has already begun living a normal life. I know he will be able to hide his disbelief from the specter.

I calmly listen to his monotonous repetition:

"A specter is haunting Europe, the specter of..."

Good Morning, Moscow!

Aﬁfter a story of mine had been broadcast on the radio, I was summoned to the All-Union Broadcasting Studio.

I was greeted by a young editor whom I had never met before. He smiled a wide, open, pro-government smile.

"We have a business offer for you," he began excitedly. "We would be happy to work with you more. Could you provide us with your content on a regular basis?"

"With pleasure! But I am afraid that radio censoring is even more strict than in the papers..."

"Who told you that? We take anything as long as it is funny, on point, and of current interest. Regardless of personalities involved, so to speak."

"I still would like to know which topics are easier to get out to the public."

"Any! Write whatever you want! Except, maybe..." the editor considered for a moment and lowered his voice. "Except, maybe, the agricultural sector. It's a sore spot, you know... Better not to poke it. And, I figure, the food lines... and food prices..."

"A sore spot?"

"Very sore. Also, the things the stores do not carry. The shortages. Meat, vegetables... Well, you know."

"I know."

"Toiletries, glassware, furniture, children's clothing..."

"And adult clothing," I interjected.

"Yes, also adult clothing. And the quality of merchandise."

"I suppose I better not mention the industry at all?"

"Better not."

"As if it doesn't exist?"

"Yes."

"Same as agriculture?"

"Yes. And no alcoholism issue, either."

"Is that also a sore spot?"

"Yes. Temporarily, of course. But... better not."

"Not to poke?"

"Not to poke. Nothing about sex, naturally. Not a word. Nowadays, you understand..."

"I know. Better not to poke."

"Absolutely. Do not touch politics, either. Customer service is boring — bribes, favoritism... Nothing on healthcare or crime, please."

"What about stupidity?"

"Whose stupidity?" the editor perked up, alert.

"A plumber's."

"Feel free. Unless he is a member of a communist labor team, or a town council member, or his photo is on honorable display at the community center."

"Great! Point taken."

"I'm glad you understand. We shall expect your new stories. On point and of current interest. Regardless of personalities involved, so to speak."

I came home and got straight to work: I sat at my desk, picked up a pen, arranged paper and books, and... did my English lessons.

The Doors are Closing

That's how they warn passengers in the Moscow subway. They care about people: plan your move, don't get your body parts stuck in the doors, have enough time to enter or exit. This is very noble. The passengers certainly would not figure it out without a special announcement. And, should something happen — they have been warned!

Moscow has a great subway. It's like a museum. It contains the history of the country: the commissars at the Revolution Square; athletes in gym shorts at the Dinamo; industrial and agricultural achievements laid out in mosaic tile on the ceiling of Mayakovsky Square... All the periods of the state's development are present.

...During each period there were instances when the doors slid open a crack. The smart ones squeezed in. The others deliberated:

"Who knows if it's going to be any better."

"We can't just leave everything behind!"

"They won't harm me, I'm one of them."

"We can always catch the next train!"

But those trains did not run as often as the ones in the Moscow subway. It was difficult to tell when the next one would stop by. So, people stayed, and waited — and not in particularly comfortable conditions. They had been warned: "Attention! The doors are closing!" — but they chose to wait at the station the size of a whole country. They are getting ready; they are waiting for their train; on different platforms, different tracks.

They will go different ways from the same station. How do they hate this station!

In every period, people left in different manners. Some in carts, some in cattle cars, some in international luxury carriages, some by Aeroflot Airlines.

In every period, those who remained stayed to die, spiritually or bodily.

"Someone should have made us leave!"

"Someone should have pushed us against our will!"

"If only we hadn't had a choice!"

Do you have a choice, though? Aren't you being pushed? Is there any other way?

"Attention! The doors are closing!"

"Maybe they will stay open? Maybe something will break? Maybe the engineer dies?"

"They'll hire another one. A worse one. He'll close the doors without warning."

"Nonsense. It will be okay. I wish we could go take a peek and then return... The doors will close on either side... I read somewhere that an animal born in captivity cannot survive in the wild. It either lacks the instincts, or reflexes, or something. Just like us. We are adapted, we are alright, we are living. Maybe if it gets too unbearable..."

"Is it still bearable now?"

"It is. Why not? We are little people. We live quietly. We don't harm anyone. We know our place. We don't stick our noses into politics. We don't do anything illegal. We would even join the Party, if we are told to. As long as there is peace and quiet..."

You'll have your peace and quiet. When the doors close, it will be so quiet that no one will hear you scream. No one will see your eyes, full of astonishment and tears.

Before it is too late!

While the doors are still open!

...The monotonous voice in the Moscow subway repeats its warning: "Attention! The doors are closing!"

P.S.: *I wrote this "warning" as soon as I emigrated from the USSR in 1978. It was published in the New York paper New Russian Word. The paper would sometimes sneak its way into the Soviet Union. Once I received a letter from Kharkiv. The woman wrote that "Attention! The doors are closing!" helped her make the decision to emigrate. In 1981 the doors closed, and those who waited too long found themselves refuseniks for many years. Nowadays, people run from Russia as they ran from the USSR in the late '70s and from Russia in the early '90s. The feeling that the doors are slowly closing, the opening is getting narrower, and you may not make it, is back. That which was written dozens of years ago is again current. I have not been to Moscow in a long time and I don't know if they still say "Attention! The doors are closing!" But this warning is in the air. It floats up from the Moscow subway getting louder and clearer. Can't you hear?*

There were several large ways of Soviet/Russian emigration. The first one happened at the time of the Bolshevik Revolt of 1917 and the subsequent Russian Civil War (Lenin). The second one fell upon the time of WWII and the early post-war years (Stalin). The third wave—Jewish—was in the 1970–80s (Brezhnev). The fourth one, in the 1990s (Yeltsin). And in the first quarter of the 21st century the fifth way began (Putin).

Before Leaving, Turn Off the Lights

Every building there carries a slogan or reminder of some sort: "To report a fire, call..."; "We shall fulfill the Government's order!"; "Warning: Construction Zone!"; "Close the valves!"; "Do not walk on grass!"; "No entry!"; "Littering unlawful!"; "Wash your hands!"; "Before leaving, turn off the lights!".

Turn off the lights. Before leaving.

All the furniture is gone. The keys are surrendered. You turn off the lights and walk out — into the darkness, into the unknown, leaving behind another unknown and another darkness, your past.

Your friends will still look up at your window when passing by. But the window will be dark. They will, on occasion, dial your phone number. But your voice will not be there. Then, gradually... you will vanish into the darkness from them; as they will also — from you.

The lights go off in another window. And another. And another. There are more and more of these windows — hundreds, thousands, tens of thousands.

I've heard Jews over there challenged construction workers to a competition: who will provide more vacant apartments to the state.

The buildings stand, and among the evening lights there are black abysses of those windows, like screaming mouths; their scream is silent. For some this scream is a war cry; for others, a cry of pain.

But the windows will not remain dark long and the apartments — empty. Too many of those in need, and they rejoice at finally receiving what they have dreamed about. They put in their own light bulbs. They turn on their lights. They have their own light. You have yours. How long will they have theirs? Is yours actually your own?

Now they have your apartment. They have very similar furniture. Their problems are similar. They have similar thoughts, too: "Shall we turn off the lights and leave? Is the light brighter elsewhere?" This light bulb is too dim. They cannot see the truth by its light.

There is a new light in your window. A brighter bulb. Too bright, perhaps. You can see the roaches and the cracks in the plaster. Nothing is as you wanted and believed it would be. You never thought it would hurt at first.

More and more often you remember that window and that light that you would have liked to bring with you. You could have used the bulb from there, here, thinking it would be better. But no, it would have been worse. So much worse that you would again hear: "Before leaving, turn off the lights."

Enough is enough! You left, you slammed the door behind you, so do not look back. It is dark there. Your light is here. You do not like being a visitor, you want to be the host. You want the light to be on when you return home. You want someone to be waiting, someone who belongs with you. And the books that belong, and the table, and the bed. This is home. You are home. Do not leave anymore. Do not close the valves, do not turn anything off. You will be back, and soon. You will be home.

Moscow to New York

O ver there, they say: "Better to rat someone out than share a cell with rats."

I was incapable of ratting anyone out, and I did not want to live with rats.

I chose the third option. I lived like the majority — saying one thing while thinking a different one. Occasionally, I said what I thought — in the company of two or three friends. Even then, I looked over my shoulder. Every day, for years.

The entire country is mentally disturbed. The diagnosis is Multiple Personality Disorder. Well, it doesn't even have a personality, so it's a Multiple Impersonality Disorder.

"So-and-so left!"

"And so did his cousin!"

"And his aunt!"

"And her daughter-in-law!"

"And their grandparents!"

"How about you?"

"I don't know... I'm still thinking. It's a hard decision."

You are in a vacuum, and there is nobody to fill it. You are tired of the overcrowded subway, of your drunk friends, of angry people on the bus, and of the customer service whose slogan is:"Don't like it? Go fly a kite!"

And you would very much like to go — to ride, to drive, or to fly.

"Are you crazy?! You have a place here, a job, a paycheck, a car... And you don't even have to work much for it. And you are no worse off than others! What more could you want?"

I'd give it all up. I'd trade my apartment, my car, my job, my paycheck, my coat, my pants, my slippers, and my underwear for permission to leave. I'd be naked yet free.

The more they deny me, the more I want it.

Ah, the encounters at the synagogue on Sabbath!

"Have you applied yet?"

"Of course. It's been three months."

"Three? You're a newbie. I've been waiting nine months. And that guy with a beard — it's been two years for him!"

"Which one? Everyone here wears a beard."

"The white beard."

The longer you wait, the whiter the beard and sadder the eyes. Experience is gained. I could share the experience and the wait.

"Hey, hello there! Are you still here?"

"Obviously."

"Wanna hang out?"

"I can't. I have Hebrew class today."

"Tomorrow?"

"Tomorrow too."

"The day after?"

"A farewell party."

"How about Saturday?"

"Synagogue."

"Sunday?"

"English class."

"I see. Alright, then. See you at the airport!"

A farewell, and a hope to see each other *over there*.

A farewell, and no hope.

Everything is for the last time. Nevermore.

"Don't forget to write!"

So, I write.

As the song goes, "I dream of the past no more, and I have no regrets."

I do, though. I do have regrets.

It's like a play by Chekhov: they sit in the garden for four acts talking — talking about leaving. But they never leave.

I do have regrets. I should have left in the first act. But the play isn't over yet. The main scene has not been performed.

The set changed, the location changed.

...New York.

"Do you like it here? Do you regret leaving there?" is the greeting for the freshly arrived.

Their responses differ. Some miss Kiev. Some dream of Odessa.

Bad things are quickly forgotten: the fear to say something wrong, to bribe the wrong person, or not to bribe the right person enough; the askance glances of the boss. Everything bad is forgotten: why they left, what they left; sitting on a powder keg. They forget random petitions of random groups of working people; the ever-threatening conscription, evacuation, expropriation... They forget.

They do not forget their childhood; the place where everything happened for the first time. They are annoyed by that which they cannot understand.

"What kind of language is this? Can't they speak like normal people, so we understand? What kind of buildings are these? What kind of subway? What is up with their laws?"

And they sigh heavily.

"I had such a nice place in Chernivtsi! Pretty as a picture! And the balcony! You know the balcony I had? I could see everything! I would take a chair to the balcony in the morning. I could see everyone and everyone could see me. Everyone said hello. Everyone brought something—the pension, or their respect. The pension was small, but the respect was big. My son-in-law was a butcher. Do you know what a butcher in Chernivtsi is? The most important man! An artist! We had meat on the table every day, and nearly free. And what meat that was! The only other place that had such meat was the Kremlin. Or maybe even they didn't. He was lucky not to get arrested. What would they have arrested him for? They steal too. Everyone there is a thief. And what thieves! He would have never been arrested. They got meat from him, and some change for vodka. Ah, if it had not been for the children..."

And they sigh heavily.

"I was a dentist back home. I was an important man! I'm nobody here. I am drek, garbage. I could pull all their teeth with my eyes closed! But they won't let me. They say I have no language. Why do I need to speak? I have eyes that see and hands that don't shake. Give me the forceps and watch! They are afraid all the patients will flock to me. So they made up an exam. Tell me whom to give cash and how much and I will pass your exam with an "A"!.. I wish I could go back..."

And they sigh heavily. They look back. They do not see ahead. They forget that if you climb up high you shouldn't look down or you will fall. They look down. They fall. They hit the ground and get strokes, heart attacks, and paralysis.

They are treated. They receive cash benefits and food stamps. Welfare checks come more often than letters from family. They get invited to celebrations and to concerts and...

They do not see. They do not see this wonderful country where they can actually live their life — the country that cares.

Lift your gaze. Step over the bag of trash. See the blooming lilac. Be amazed.

Touch a coconut. Buy a mango without waiting in an endless line. Pinch yourself where it's most sensitive — and be amazed.

Read the "pros" and "cons" on the walls. Do not be neutral. Say what you think, if you have someone to talk to.

Go to the airport. Greet someone there. Be amazed.

Look around. See the new life, and not the government-sponsored news.

Look at yourself in the mirror. Be amazed. Your chin doesn't tremble. Your hands are not in fists. Your posture is straight. Your belly is round.

Look at your children who are happy and want all of this. Look at your grandchildren babbling in English. Be amazed.

Fall in love. Fall in love with your Forest Hills and your Brighton Beach and your velvety Manhattan. Fall in love with these sly curly-haired tricksters whom you lost fifteen dollars to. Fall in love with these nice guys who want you to buy something or stop by someplace.

Fall in love with this bridge across the Universe at night, full of lights and clamor.

Fall in love with these colorful girls on these colorful streets.

Fall in love with this patchwork union of states.

It is yours. It is for you. It stretches its arms out towards you. Stretch out your arms towards it. Love each other. And be happy.

And Prison for All

I was reading a Russian paper on the subway. A tiny unpresentable old man was sitting next to me. Curious, he kept looking over my shoulder, fidgeting, and distracting me. In situations like this I always want to give the restless person a page or two of my reading material, so that each of us is entertained. I was about to do just that when the old man said in Polish: "Are you from Russia, sir?"

"I am," I responded in kind.

We started talking. I did know a bit of Polish, and he spoke some Russian.

"God does not love us, Poles, no sir," he kept saying. "Why is it that our Poland has Germany on one side and Russia on the other?"

He told me about his time at a Nazi prison camp and of everything he had endured: torture, starvation, and the death of his wife. Then came the Russians who "liberated" him and promptly sent him to Siberia.

"My daughter perished in Siberia. She was still little."

With his daughter gone, he was alone. Later, he was "rehabilitated"; they said it all had been a mistake, and, as a Polish citizen, he was allowed to leave the Soviet Union. However, he could not stay in the Communist Poland, either. It was a different country from the one he had lived in and loved before the war. That's how he ended up in America.

"I know very well what Siberia is, what Communism is," he said.

I rent an apartment in Williamsburg, Brooklyn. Hungarian hasidim live here. Soon after I moved here, I walked into a shop and tried to speak to the shop owner in my terrible English. Somehow he immediately guessed I was from the Soviet Union and said in Russian: "Speak Russian. I understand good."

"How?" I was surprised.

"Hiding me from Nazis I ran to Soviets. Soviets hid me good — in Magadan's labor camp... *Tvoju mat'... Balanda... Zhidovska morda...*"*

The hasid said these words with a smile, proud to show off his Russian vocabulary.

In New York, I made friends with a family from Romania. Jorji and his wife are always happy to host and their table is always laid for good friends. Old Jorji likes to tell tales:

"I was young, I loved to sing and wanted to be an actor. I knew that Moscow, in the Soviet Union, had the best Yiddish theater. I was young and stupid. I went to Moscow to study at a theater school. I studied, and I was funny, and I told jokes. Suddenly Russians arrested me and said I was an American spy. The Soviet investigator beat me in the right side of my head with a rubber baton. "Comrade chief, why are you neglecting my left hemisphere? It is not fair. You disturb the balance." The investigator laughed and said: 'I'm doing it on purpose. If you live, you will always have a headache and you will remember me.' He was right, that investigator. I haven't forgotten him in forty years."

I recall encounters in Moscow and conversations at the doors of the Visa and Passport Agency where those wishing to emigrate filed their paperwork. Once, I saw an ancient, shabbily dressed woman. Her dark wrinkled face resembles dry cracked mud. The woman eagerly told everyone that she was Greek and had come to visit a niece in Kuban region, North Caucasus. She stayed for three months and now wanted to go back to Greece, but wasn't allowed to.

"How's that?" the crowd wondered. "Don't you have a passport?"

---

* Russian slang words for "f*** your mother", "gruel", "ugly Jew-face".

The old woman unwrapped a filthy rag and showed them her Greek passport.

"How can they keep you here, then? Why?"

The old woman said that she had been born in Russia. Her small ethnic group had from time immemorial lived in Crimea, in the North Caucasus, around the Azov Sea, and in Odessa. Later, however, they suffered the same fate as the Volga Germans, Crimean Tatars, and many other ethnic minorities of the Soviet Union. Only the Greeks were much less known and nobody had so far said a word in their defense.

"When I lost my parents and then my husband, I decided to leave Russia. A few of us escaped to Bessarabia. Long time ago, it was. Now the policeman keeps me here and says: "You, old hag, will receive your pension here. The same you had in Greece. Only in rubles.""

The stubborn woman did not want to stay, so she was fighting to go home.

On the same spot by the Agency I met an Iranian. He was trying to obtain permission to visit his brother in Iran. He was a communist who had escaped persecution and ran to the USSR in the late 1950s. He settled in Soviet Azerbaijan.

"We Iranians are plentiful there," he said.

He had a strange passport—stateless. When he left Iran, he lost his Iranian citizenship, and either never accepted or had been denied Soviet citizenship. Now he complained to me that the Agency refused to grant him a visitor's permit. "If you want to go, leave for good!" He was told. "No, I can't leave for good. I have a wife and children here. They are Soviet citizens. Will you let them leave?" "Of course not. So, stay where you are and don't stir the pot!" was the answer. What could he do? Now he was going from one government official to another, begging.

"I never thought it would be this way... I never... I wish I had known..."

When I saw my first emigrant friends off at the Sheremetyevo Airport, I noticed a large group of simply but neatly dressed country people. The men wore wrinkled caps, the women— head kerchiefs. Their faces were dark and dry from the sun of the steppes. They had light blue eyes and blond hair. They were Germans of the Volga who had been exiled to Kazakhstan. Now, thanks to an international agreement, they were emigrating to West Germany (I believe there is no need to explain why they weren't going to East Germany). These pretty much Russian people had lived on the banks of the Volga river for many generations and hundreds of years and were now abandoning their homes, the graves of their parents, and leaving. A woman of about forty brought along her elderly mother and three young children. The kids were crying. The oldest girl ran to a short slender man who had tears in his eyes. The Germans had no suitcases. They had sacks and bundles. I cannot forget their village folk faces and their eyes, full of eternal suffering.

I saw repatriated Armenians. Long ago they decided to return to their ancestral land and came to Soviet Armenia from France and Greece and Lebanon and America. They were well off and brought their riches to Armenia. Now, I saw them at Sheremetyevo. They were leaving home again. This time, probably, forever.

Faded red banners with the sacred Soviet slogans of "peace, labor, freedom, equality, brotherhood, and happiness for all people" cover the many cracks in the apartment buildings in Moscow. Words, all empty words...

I heard a joke in Bulgaria. A Russian and a Bulgarian found hidden treasure. The Russian says: "Well, buddy, let's split it as brothers would!" "No thank you," says the Bulgarian. "Let's split it fairly."

Everywhere I go in New York, I meet people who had personally "enjoyed" the heavy hand of their Soviet "brothers". I meet people of different ethnicities and different nationalities united by the Soviet prison — a prison for all.

Sad Melody

Roads, oh roads...
The dust and the mists,
The cold and the worries,
And the tumbleweeds.

A Russian song

The black raven of memory circles at night, flies into dreams and brings familiar faces from the past on his wings.

They are there.

You are here.

Many are those who would like to do as you did! But they cannot.

Many are those who would write! But they do not.

Many are those of whom you think and whom you talk to in your head!

They are there.

You are here.

You have been born again.

They are getting older.

You think: enough, it's time to forget! You will never see them again, never sit down at a table, never talk, never be silent together...

They keep silent without you. They don't talk. They keep their mouths shut.

You had enough of that. You got out. You speak. But... in a foreign language that you barely understand. So, which is better? To be silent in your own language or speak in a strange one? Doesn't their silence speak? Aren't your words silent?

Everything is great here. Everything is here. If only you could also have your friends! And the Moscow of your childhood. And the Hermitage and the Russian Museum. And Suzdal. And the Khreshchatyk!..

You cannot forget what you ran from. You cannot forget the insults and the meanness. But you cannot forget the kindness, either: the moments of joy in the joyless time.

You do not want to go back. You want to phone and say: "Hey guys. Here I am, alive and well. I'm doing great." You want to say that out loud, in Russian. And you want to hear a response in Russian: "Hey man! Good to hear your voice. Same old, same old here. Wanna drop by?"

And you drop by; the friends gather — all that saw you off at the airport and even those who didn't risk it — many old friends. Old friends and old wine are the best. A sack of salt together... Break the bread... Give them your coat...

Is it a moment of weakness or a test of strength? Or, perhaps, just a memory. Just an old song. You have to take the good with the bad — the old bad makes the new good complete.

> Through snow or wind,
> Remember, my friends —
> Roads like these
> No one forgets.

An Immigrant and Tzimmes

Americans believe that on a holiday evening, nobody should be alone. I would add that nobody should be alone on any other evening, either.

A new immigrant was invited to a holiday dinner with an American family. "We have to introduce these Russians into our life," they thought. "We must make them feel at home."

He was invited, so he showed up. A dog with an odd name Tzimmes greeted him with joyful barking. The hostess chattered in English. The host, with great care, helped the guest out of his coat.

The guest sat where he was pointed and accepted a wine glass. Now he was supposed to hold a conversation. That was something he couldn't do. "Damn English," he thought, guessing at what was being said and pretending to understand. He laughed when everybody laughed. His face became serious when everyone else's faces did. However, the game soon exhausted him. He wanted to be understood and to talk heart to heart. He suffered from his muteness and begged for help. The help arrived in the form of Tzimmes. The dog approached the guest, sniffed the human's leg, stood on his hind legs, put his front paws in the guest's lap and looked the man in the eyes. How alike were they at that moment — two creatures lacking the gift of speech. Still, Tzimmes had some skills that the man did not possess. The dog could express himself through his eyes, his bark, his wagging tail, or a whine. The guest could not dare do any of that. It is not considered polite among humans to whine, bark, or wag tails. So, the man, trapped in a three-piece suit and a tie that was attempting to strangle him, suffered quietly. Tzimmes understood everything but could not speak. The man could neither speak nor understand.

The host decided to demonstrate Tsimmes's abilities to the guests. He showed the dog a piece of meat and began giving commands. Tzimmes, eyes on the treat, lay down, sat, stood on his hind legs, crawled, and almost danced — all just for a piece of meat. And the commands were in English! Tzimmes would understand them even if the language was that of clapping.

The guest envied Tzimmes. Not because of the meat itself, but because the dog had worked for the treat and earned it. The man had studied this doggone English at school, then with a tutor, and now in an ELL class, and all to no avail!

Tzimmes felt bad for the man. He ate his well-earned piece of meat, but felt kind of awkward about it. The dog came up to the man and lay at his feet to show his friendship and understanding. He did not lay at the feet of his master who gave him meat, but at the feet of a man new to America, helpless and alone, like a stray dog. The guest was grateful for the dog's consideration, for his solidarity. And Tzimmes fully realized his responsibility for this inexperienced stranger who could not even bark to express himself.

That holiday night the immigrant felt a little less lonely.

Small Joys

Oh those small joys, the small joys of a small immigrant.

The phone rings in the morning. Life calls. And you run, knocking chairs over. Does someone really need you? Does someone really know you exist? It may be something trivial, maybe even a wrong number. But it is a contact with the world! You are on the line, you are ready! It is the first of today's cracks in your solitary confinement.

You devour your toast and run downstairs, keys jingling. Your heart is skipping steps along with your feet. Here is the magic door to the world of communication — your mailbox. What if there is a letter?! You feel with every fiber that it is there. It must be. You felt it yesterday too, but not as strongly. That's why it wasn't there yesterday. It will be there today! There! There is one! It is a power bill. Here's another one, the natural gas bill. They do remember you! They do know you! They do need you! Con Edison takes constant care of you! It is a small joy, but it is a joy.

You run to the subway. You have brought a few coins from home — for the newspaper, a Russian newspaper that you buy from a Mexican on the corner. You thank him. You hurry into the train, sit down comfortably, and read and read on a long ride. You dive into the sea of information and doggy paddle through it from shore to shore. How beautiful is the world! How many robberies, murders, revolts, floods, and earthquakes! But you are alive! Despite everything, you are living! It's a button-size joy, but here it is — the joy of being!

And these awesome classifieds that let you buy anything and sell it right away! There you go: buy a coffee shop and treat your friends for free. Buy a house in the mountains or on a beach. Is it expensive? So what? The point is not whether you can or can't afford it. The point is, you could buy it. If you had the money, you totally could!

Everything is here: you can get a babysitting job; have your erectile dysfunction healed by a witch; pile your scrap gold on the counter of a pawn; utilize the services of a mortuary. And, as a newcomer, you get discounts. They do care about you! They do need you! They do expect you! It is a small and quiet joy, but it is a joy.

Here the Tolstoy Foundation is seeking... You? About an inheritance? No, your name isn't there. Maybe tomorrow, or the day after. Someday they will find you for sure! They can't fail to. Because you exist; you are here!

You hurry to the places where people are — classes or work. What? How? Where? How much? Who has arrived? How are they settling in? Not great? Pretty bad? That's good! It means somebody is worse off than you. A little joy. A small one, a tiny one, but a joy nevertheless.

And these strong policemen in the subway on your way home! You feel so brave when you see them. You feel ready to defend someone weak, to punish someone rude. The policeman is already doing it, but you could! If it wasn't your stop. You made it home, safe and sound. You were protected. It's a joy!

But the biggest joy is still ahead! It is a small box, noisy and winking. It waits. It thinks about you. If it could, it would turn itself on ahead of time. It wags its antenna like a tail, happy to see you. It is happy, and you are happy. You are both happy. These little joys shine in millions of windows. They flow together and form one immense little joy, huge like New York City, small, like you — curled up in the corner, snuffling and smiling in your sleep.

A Tale of a Tail

"Hello. I evolved from an ape. But I got my stuff together, changed the climate zone, and now I'm becoming a man."

I began realizing where I had come from as a grade school
student. Remember a picture in the biology book? A man fully
covered with hair. He was Russian, one Andrian Evtikheev. Not
a Johnson, not a Rivera. His origins were obvious. They were
plain on his face, so to speak. There was also another picture —
a naked boy with a short tail.

The thing that wasn't quite clear from these pictures was
whether an ape was turning into a man, or a man into an ape.
This question has bothered me since I was a child. I was afraid
I was devolving. It turns out, I had reasons to be afraid.

During puberty certain signs began to develop. I would grab
at every opportunity to find myself up high. I made faces at the
command of my superiors. My herd instinct developed: one for
all and all for one.

Moreover, I noticed that I was not the only one turning into
an ape. When an older apelike female yelled: "Be ready to fight
for the cause of Lenin and Stalin!", we would all respond: "Always ready!" What that cause was and what the ways to fight
for it were, we didn't even consider. We didn't have the considering organ in our body. We were turning into apes, and the
signs were plain on our faces.

Of course, we did our best to conceal those signs. We shaved
the hair, cut it, and plucked it out. We tied off the tails with
string, had them surgically removed, camouflaged them, and

covered them with slogans... All in vain. The signs rapidly developed, stimulated by the environment. Still, it did not stop many of us from being members of the Party and trade unions, from holding official positions and climbing the career ladder. The curious thing was that the further one moved from human towards ape, the higher was the position. They did not care what they were; they would turn into kangaroos to be able to fill their pouches. Others gave up and became apes. Such was their fate. Yet others wanted to remain human. They were the ones to realize that, first of all, the environment had to change. Some waited for change at home; others took the initiative and changed their homes, cities, countries, and hemispheres.

I, too, changed the hemisphere. And guess what? Under the influence of a new environment the outward signs of the ape began to slowly disappear. "Great," I thought, "I am healed!" Now I could go out in public. So I did.

"Hello," I said. "I came from an ape. But I made an effort and changed my environment. Now I'm becoming a man. How about you?"

"Ohhh," they respond, "we changed the environment before we turned into apes, as soon as we felt it coming."

"Aha!" I thought. "The Civil War in Russia. The White Guard. Counterrevolution!" And I felt my concealed tail wagging and my armpits itching. The signs were back. No, I said to myself, it is too early for me to be out in public. Too early.

I isolated myself. I enjoyed sunbathing. Soon I felt an amazing ease. My back straightened. My brow became wider and more pronounced. The widow peak appeared as a sign of the impending arrival of brain power.

I decided to go out into the world again.

"Hello," I said. "I came from an ape, but I changed the environment, and now I am a man. And you?"

"Yes, us too! But we did it much earlier, at the time of the Great Fight of Two Whiskered Apes. We changed the environment at the first opportunity."

"Aha!" I thought. "The Second World War. *Polizei*. Traitors!"

And I felt my tail squirm and my armpits itch. The signs were back.

I was angry, so I became a hermit again. I drank herbal teas and medicinal potions. I lived under the sky, exposed to the influence of my new environment. One day I looked at my reflection in a puddle and marveled. There was no hair. My skin was smooth. My head was bald. My body had no blemish — not only the tail, but all the freckles had disappeared. I was a real human!

So, I went out into the world!

"We too," they responded. "used to be apes. We were born and raised in a zoo. Then we decided to change the environment. Now we are humans."

So they spoke, while looking at me askance and scratching their armpits.

"Aha!" it dawned on me. "They are my contemporaries. Spies. Snitches. Agents." And I began to scratch my armpits. The signs were there.

What in the world? I could not heal from this. I lived in a good climate zone, among humans, and my life should have been determining my thinking. And yet... My thinking was still back in the zoo.

I didn't have a visible tail. But inside, the tail was long. We ran from the zoo, but stayed there. The body was that of a human, but the soul was still applying for emigration.

Let the soul reunite with the body! Let the boy lose his tail!

Stanislavski's System

Once, a provincial actor met his counterpart. One was Russian, from Saratov, the other American, from Philadelphia. Of course, there is no such thing as a "provincial actor" in America; it's just "an actor". They talked about Stanislavski's system that teaches actors to perform realistically, as if in real life, so the spectators would believe.

The American said: "Explain to me this Stanislavski's system. Not in fancy words, but in a simple way, with real life examples. I want to understand every element of it."

"That is a difficult task, " the Russian replied. "I can only do it briefly and very simplified. Okay. So. Let's take one element of the system — imagination, the Magic If. For example, what can you imagine?"

"Me? Well... I won a million dollars..."

"Alright. And then?"

"I invested it into a profitable business and made two million."

"And then?"

"Then I made a few more millions."

"And?"

"Then I lived off the interest, without a care in the world."

"Great! I do have to tell you, though, that American imagination loses to Russian."

"What does a Russian actor dream of?"

"Oh! I dream of a full-time job on TV, leading three amateur drama clubs, and in a couple of years, a car..."

"And then?"

"And then I can go shopping in Moscow."

"Whoa!"

"What did you expect? Real imagination must be on a large scale. Here's another one. You guys don't imagine that you are free; we do. We also pretend that we work, and our government pretends that we make money. We pretend that we build a bright future for all mankind, and you can't even imagine what it is and how it may end."

"True, we Americans ought to learn imagination from Russians."

"To fully convince you, here's another example. Our leader meets yours. Ours says that he is for world peace, that there are no political prisoners in our country, that we do not interfere in other countries' affairs, and that we are generally good. He says all that and pretends that it really is so. He even gets emotional — that's how good he is. That's what it means to act on Stanislavski's system!"

"How does our leader act?" asked the American.

"Yours? That leads us to the next element of the system — belief in given circumstances. Your leader is way ahead of ours on this one. Ours makes up the circumstances, and yours believes in them."

"Okay. Let's leave the actors from the capitals alone and go back to your regular normal actors and their belief in given circumstances."

"We Russians have much better developed imagination — our entire life is pretend play, but you Americans are ahead of us in belief."

"Like what?"

"Like this. If Russian TV says that Russian people are living better and happier, the people smile sardonically. They don't believe it. They don't believe in a bright future for all mankind or even one country. They don't. That's why they steal and drink. Sometimes two people talk and do not believe each other. There is no belief."

"It's the opposite with us. Sometimes they believe so much that... The next leader promises to eliminate poverty and unemployment, to conquer inflation, to solve the problem of inequality, to stop global warming... And we believe him and vote for him. Then we are disappointed when he cannot do what he promised.”

“I see you have figured this one out. Now let's move on to 'organic silence'. I think Russians can do silence more organically than Americans. This is because of...”

“Given circumstances.”

“Given by whom?”

“By system”

“Which system?”

“Stanislavsky of cours.”

“Excellent!”

“You Russians are brilliant actors. You can remain silent for years! For centuries! We Americans are still learning. It is against our nature. It's not organic to us, yet.”

“Yeah, you are still weak in that regard. I'm glad you realize that. Alright, we have this element figured out. Moving on to the “Attitude toward a object'.”

“What is that?”

“I'll try to explain. There is an object in front of you. For example, a bone. You must see it as meat. Get it?”

“No, I don't. I can see that it is a bone, not meat. How can I see it as...”

“You can't? The entire Russian population can. The whole crowd, the whole extras. Only the main actors see meat but treat it as a bone and say that they are with the people. Here's another example. You are a literary critic. You read Brezhnev's *The Virgin Lands* and treat it as *The Idiot*.”

“It is difficult for us Americans to understand. If a car is bad, we can't see it as good. If we do, we will get into a crash.”

“We don't crash. Everything is seemingly bad: the body is rusted, there are no spare parts, the tires are worn out, the brakes don't work... Only a banner waves merrily. At least until it also gets stolen. Still, we are rolling! We are actors! We see an old soviet car Zaporozhets as a new Volkswagen. This is the mysterious Russian soul and Stanislavski's system! Let's move on to the part about communication and interaction.”

"Here we, Americans, are surely ahead."

"No doubt. But it is not because Russians don't like interacting with people, but rather because they can't."

"How so?"

"They're not allowed. One can get arrested for having 'foreign connections'."

"How is that a bad thing? People connect and learn and understand one another and live in peace. That's what communication is for."

"Well, in Russia they see it differently. Before a Russian actor group goes abroad, they are warned by political instructors to avoid interaction with the natives. No communication."

"Why?"

"Such contact may be contagious, and a Russian will catch freedom of thought! They cannot allow such contact. It's much better to give Russians a bottle of vodka so they can drink it in their hotel room and interact all they want with Russian snitches. A bottle of vodka is the heart of Russian interaction. Vodka is the basis for mutual understanding and respect."

"What about communication within your own country?"

"Communicate away! But not too much... There are some who like interacting in public, like in a bread line. There is always a grumpy old woman who curses the government and says that she has nothing to lose. The people around her pretend to be deaf and mute, but there is approving laughter in their eyes—they communicate like that. If you want to be left alone, though, you're better off not interacting with anybody. Total isolation."

"That's why Americans are ahead in communication skills."

"Sure. But you are far behind in performing without an object."

"Is it some kind of pantomime?"

"Kind of. And here we will never let you get ahead. In ancient Russia, they used to build with just an ax and not a single nail. We still do it. There is even some improvement: we can build without the ax. Often there are no nails and no axes. And no shovels. Either everything has been stolen, or a production line stopped, or the entire shop got drunk, or the factory roof caved in. So, we have to perform without an object. Our entire people have mastered this art. Every time there is an object missing. The famous actors from the capital are the biggest masters: they pretend that we have no shortages and the people are satisfied. However, if the people stop pretending to be happy, the pantomime will end and the performance will gain objects."

"Considering your 'organic silence' this will not happen any time soon. You don't have a real director, either... What's the next element?"

"Attention. You and us differ on that one also. When you are looking at a painting, what are you thinking?"

"If I like the painting, I look at it for a long time. I enjoy the colors, the subject, the artist's skill, the light and shadow... Sometimes I don't exactly know what it is I like. I just like it. If painting does not interest me, I walk past it."

"We do it differently. We concentrate our attention not on 'how' but on 'what it is about'. Does it serve a goal or not? It may be badly painted, but it demonstrates a purpose, is politically correct, and current, like the painting *A Comrade from Moscow Among Workers of Novorossiysk*. A painting like that deserves special attention from the media and the critics. And in this case, criticism is not criticism, but flowing honey."

"So, what is 'attention'?"

"Attention, according to Stanislavski, is looking and seeing and listening and hearing."

"Every normal human does that."

"Normal, maybe, but not Russians. We are taught to look but not see, to listen but not hear. We look at the incredible harvests on TV, but do not see them in the stores. We listen to speeches on the radio about unprecedented improvement in workers' standard of living, but we do not hear. We had stopped believing a long time ago... Well, we already covered belief."

"What else is in this system?"

"Lots of things. Here is a curious part — to become someone else while remaining yourself. This you Americans have to learn from us, and learn, and learn again — as the great teacher Lenin said. Russia is full of pretend personalities. Sometimes we even overdo it. We become someone else so well that we forget how to be ourselves. This condition is born from the fear of being exposed and to say what you think. You have to be able to look sincere while being insincere. A person can be a snitch while not conforming in his heart. He can be a Party activist while remaining politically indifferent in his heart. That's real performing art!"

"Fascinating! I can now conclude that you Russians are much better actors than us. You follow a system. We just play, like children."

"The system is a great thing! Our system is gaining more and more supporters. Long live... I'll tell you in confidence, though: we wish to live outside the system, to live like children; to live and not to perform on stage..."

"What about Stanislavski's system?"

"It is only good for theater."

A Russian Jew Uncertain

THERE: "You are not Russian. You look like a Jew!"
HERE: "How can you be Jewish when you are Russian?"

There, I was a Jew and an alien.
I left there to stop being an alien and remain a Jew.
I came here to become Russian and still be an alien.
I had to leave Russia to become Russian.
"What are you?"
"A Jew."
"Are you circumcised?"
"No."
"Do you go to synagogue?"
"No."
"Do you speak Hebrew?"
"No."
"Do you know Yiddish?"
"No."
"Do you observe the Sabbath?"
"No."
"Do you know your people's history?"
"No."
"What's your last name?"
"Ivanov."
"How can you be a Jew?"
There, I was a Jew pretending to be Russian.
Here, I am a Jew pretending to be Russian pretending to be American.

When you wear so many masks your whole life, you forget your own face.

What archeologist will find the original layer after clearing off the more recent ones?

"Hello?" Call out the various faces of myself in search of wholeness.

"Hello?" Comes back the echo of the question.

Echo does not provide an answer. Where to find the answer? There? Here? Somewhere else? That is why I cannot sit still. You could live three or four hundred years in a strange house hoping the answer is there, hoping that a strange house can become yours.

So you begin to paint, fix, and patch. Now the roof does not leak, and the porch is decorated with wood carving, and the curtains are fluttering on the windows. How pretty! A sight for sore eyes! You have done everything; now you can enjoy life.

"Are you done here? What are you waiting for? Go, friend. Now we can manage without you."

And you go out into the world again, a transient laborer.

"But you now have your own home, with your own kin!"

"I do. And I am tempted to go there. But something won't let me. Uncertainty. They say: "Next year in Jerusalem!" But if I am already in Jerusalem, where am I next year? If I am already in Jerusalem, what is the goal, the dream, the symbol? Where is the Wandering Jew that makes the earth spin with his worn-out shoes? Ever walking, ever searching, ever dreaming of the next year...

What other dream, what other destination can replace the symbol of Jerusalem? Can money, villas, yachts? Doesn't thirst for wealth lead to poverty in spirit?

Uncertainty.

Are there two Jerusalems — the one that already exists and the one of the "next year"?

It's a multiple city disorder, a multiple nation disorder. Doesn't multiple personality disorder reflect that of a whole nation?

It is easier to defend yourself and to win when there are two of You. There is always someone smart to talk to.

This is the uncertainty. The uncertainty of a Russian Jew.

If to leave, where to go?

I will come. I promise. But later. Later.

They say that you can't know someone else's soul. What about your own? You want to go to one place, yet turn away and walk in a different direction, farther and farther away.

You want to be whole and indivisible, yet you divide into more and more parts. A Jew who left Russia but did not go to Israel is broken into three pieces. Eventually, there is no identity left, just tiny shards.

What glass blower will gather the shards, toss them in his oven and blow a wonderful new vessel?

The Wandering Jew travels through time and space.

Another tribe of Israel wanders. How many are those tribes? Those that have been lost.

The branch stretches farther and farther from the trunk. It withers and lives again and reaches for the sky. It thinks it exists on its own. It forgets its roots. But the root is one. The nurturing root is in the soil of the land that was promised. If you leave it, you disappear in the fog of centuries, just like those lost tribes.

The Jew walks through fields and forests, cities and countries. He walks the longest road in the world. He walks around the round planet. He goes far; he comes close. He walks away from himself; he returns to himself; but at what cost!

How much is lost along the way!

How many weak ones chose to be Gentiles among their own rather than aliens among strangers!

How many perish to persecution and compromise!

They cannot walk; they stay; they fall; they get mired...

The mesh is too fine. Too few go through it. Fewer and fewer of them can keep going.

Now, there is nothing left and none left. Everything and everyone has been swept away. The earth turned into desert. A lone Jew wanders that desert. He is exhausted and stooped; his beard flows in the wind and there is sorrow in his eyes.

This is the end.

Or is it another beginning?

A Festival

We are guests at a strangers' festival.

Every Saturday I watch nicely dressed Jews taking their nicely dressed children to the synagogue. The whole family goes. And after, at home, they will have their Sabbath meal on Sabbath tableware on a white table cloth. They are in a festive mood. They wait for the Sabbath and prepare for it all week. It finally comes Friday evening. It happens every week. It is a feast for the soul.

Every Sunday I watch nicely dressed African Americans and Hispanics take their nicely dressed children to church. The children are in their Sunday best. They walk slowly and solemnly. It is the most important event of the week. Everybody knows Sunday is a holy day. It is not only rest from labor; it is a joy, the joy of life.

I remember the life back where I am from. The people eagerly wait for Saturday and Sunday to rest from the job they hate. But even these two days bring no rest. These are laundry days, cleaning days. Sunday night they visit with friends or host friends in their home. There is a lot of drinking. Someone falls asleep, another one, and another... One sleeps in the bathroom, hugging the toilet; another has his new suit ripped in a fight and his eye blackened in an argument of who respects whom. Very festive! Monday morning, heads ache, hands shake, and faces are swollen. And inside there is nausea and disgust.

There is no holiday. No feast for the soul.

No holiday? What about eating the food you had never had before, for free? Isn't that a feast? What about actually getting to buy something after waiting in a long line? What about coming home unhumiliated and uncheated? How about coming home to a content wife? What about learning that the Party meeting the next day is canceled? What about picking up the laundry — your own, undamaged, and on time? That's a whole lot of celebrations! Every day, every hour, every minute.

This is the bright future we read about. Well, maybe, we read about something else, but we were told to think that it was about the bright future.

Feast days became ordinary. You wait for ordinary days like feast days. The ordinary days for your soul. Where are they? To quietly sit over the Holy Book. Where is it? To think your own thoughts, and to rise. None of this was back there. Holidays were replaced by a void. The void entered us and settled within. Now we carry it with us, even though we ran from it.

Now we watch the Jews and the Christians and envy them. Or pretend we don't need any of that, but instead need a better place to live, a bigger paycheck, a TV more colorful. We do need all that also. But we need a holiday more. So the soul could rejoice — on Saturday or Sunday, or Tuesday — every week, on the seventh day, as we were told to do, as the soul needs.

Then the void will be filled, and peace will come on that day. We will get rid of the vanity that is not life but only vanity. Then that which we have been seeking and for which we abandoned our kin and friends, will come. This all leads to something big. All the past, present, and future suffering is for the Feast, the feast of the soul. This festival will come; it will enter the soul — if the door is open, if the host is home and not at the bank depositing another hundred dollars. The holiday will come if you call.

A Draw

Once there lived a very smart but ugly Prince. He met a beautiful Princess and fell in love. The Princess, unfortunately, was not smart. She said: "Why would I need the love of such an ugly man?"

The Prince decided to win the Princess' heart. He wrote interesting books, built grand palaces and invented wondrous machines.

Years went by. The smart Prince and the beautiful Princess saw each other again. Only the Princess wasn't beautiful any longer: she was old, stooped, wrinkled, and had no teeth.

"See," said the smart Prince, "I may be ugly, but everyone knows me and loves me. I will always be remembered, because my creations will last centuries. Who remembers your beauty? Everyone has already forgotten."

"You are right," replied the stupid Princess. "But you forget that everything you created you created for me, for my beauty. My beauty will live as long as your creations live."

"We'll call it a draw," said the Prince.

How a Storyteller
Won Half a Kingdom

Once there lived a storyteller, and he needed a new computer, but he had no money. What was he to do? He went to the King and told him about his problem.

The King said: "I won't lend you money, but I'll let you earn it."

"How?"

"Tell me a story. I want a tale that is entirely fictional. Your kind likes to stick real life in your tales. I want a pure fairytale. Can you do that?"

"Want a bet?"

"Sure. I bet half my kingdom."

"Deal! Now, Your Highness, listen closely. Once there lived a servant. He led a modest life and worked honestly. One day he decided to buy a soccer team. So he did."

"What, just like that?"

"Yup."

"And with honest money?"

"Yup."

"That, my friend, is pure fiction."

"Correct! You owe me half a kingdom."

How I Played Actor

Nina Adamovna Buivan, the director and instructor at the Moscow Central Culture House's drama club, liked to experiment. I was fourteen when she gave me voice acting lessons; a year later she gave me Egmont's part from Goethe's play of the same name. The hero of Holland's resistance to Spanish occupation says his final words in prison, awaiting his impending execution. He calls his people to keep fighting for freedom. I, a fifteen-year-old, had to believably pretend that I was a prisoner prepared to die as a hero for my country. My instructor made arrangements with an amateur orchestra and its conductor Igor Chalyshev to have Beethoven's overture played right after my monologue.

This was supposed to help me "live" the part. Now, picture this: thirty musicians sit still on stage while a teenage amateur actor solemnly delivers a ten-minute monologue that he barely understands; then the orchestra joins in and plays for ten minutes; all this time I had to stand, unmoving, as a monument to the hero. Those ten minutes felt like an eternity. I tried hard not to even blink, let alone shift from foot to foot or scratch.

This was my acting debut.

After I graduated from Shchukin Drama College, I was accepted to the First Moscow Regional Drama Theater. Its director by the name of Benkendorf wrote a play about the trial of the American pilot who dropped an atomic bomb on Hiroshima. I was given the silent part of the chairman of the jury. To make me into an American (as the director imagined an

American should look), I, twenty-one at the time, was given a gray mustache, a cane, and my temples were dusted with gray powder. During the two acts I was supposed to pretend to listen carefully to the witnesses, the attorney for the defendant, and the prosecutor, peering closely at each one in an attempt to determine who could be trusted.

The play was boring and full of propaganda, and I had a very hard time staying put for three hours playing an American when I had never before seen an American. I did my best. This was my second acting experience.

When I moved to New York, I was invited to act in an off-Broadway play based on Peter Weiss's *The Investigation*. The play depicted the Frankfurt Auschwitz trials of the Nazi criminals who had murdered Russians, Jews, Poles, and other prisoners in death camps. According to the vision of the director Michael Bavar nearly all witnesses for the prosecution were to sit on stage and wait for their turn to speak. Since my English was bad and my Russian accent was good, I was given the part of a Russian witness.

The play lasted two and a half hours without an intermission. My three-minute part was about two hours in. The entire time before that I had to sit in the full view of the audience as a picture of the mysterious Russian soul. We performed that play every day, sometimes twice a day, for several months. It was a Chinese water torture for me.

A recent immigrant, I seized every job, attended English classes, and, with a lot on my plate, was always sleep-deprived. Can you imagine how sleepy I was during the play? To avoid dozing off, I, sitting on the witness bench facing the audience, rubbed the fingers of my left hand with my right, and the other way round, concentrating hard on one thing: not falling asleep.

The director loved me and brought me up as an example to other actors: how deep in his part this Russian was, how in character, how intensely he followed the proceedings — even his fingers spoke about it! The American actors nodded in agreement.

These three adventures in acting were more than enough. I decided to abandon playing an actor and go play a journalist instead. And the audience believed me yet again. Maybe I am not a terrible actor after all?

The Taming of the Shrew

I am a normal husband to my normal wife. I rarely argue with her. She argues with me often. I try to change her while staying loyal to her. One day, we were sitting in a Russian restaurant. In the background, a song in Russian played.

"Oh, that's Misha Shufutinsky's voice!" Sighed my wife with adoration.

"It is Misha's, but Misha Gulko's," I corrected quietly, careful to not anger my wife with the correction.

"Do you think I can't tell my Shufutinsky from your Gulko?!" She said, angrily.

"I don't think you can," I confirmed quietly, careful not to anger my wife with the confirmation.

"Want a bet I'm right?"

"If you insist."

"What do you bet?"

I considered it. What should I bet to convince her I was right without actually betting anything? I scanned the menu. There it was!

"A bottle of 1992 Rose Dom Perignon Brut."

My wife hesitated for a moment, trying to guess at the price of the wine, but did not give up.

"Deal!"

We called a waiter and asked him to ask the DJ who the singer was.

The waiter returned and said: "It is Misha Gulko."

My wife sighed and, pretending to read the menu, asked warily:

"You, of course, do not have 1992 Rose Dom Perignon Brut?" She heavily emphasized the "not".

The waiter, however, did not catch her drift — not many do — and responded excitedly: "We have just received some! I'll be right back!"

He was off before my wife could think of a response.

The check arrived. I passed it on to my wife. You should have seen her face! The amount was astronomical. We were not even saved by the fact that we had been invited to the restaurant by a wealthy friend. He paid for the dinner, but not the champagne.

"You took the bet, pay up!" he laughed.

We told the story to Misha Gulko when we saw him next. He, an expert in wines, exclaimed to my wife: "For that kind of money I would have sang to you personally all night!"

I thought my wife had learned the lesson and would not make any bets with me anymore. How naive I was!

Some time later, my wife and I had an argument about female attractiveness. My wife quoted Russian actress Faina Ranevskaya: "I have never been beautiful, but I have always been damn cute." Then she continued:

"I know I was never the girl of your dreams. You searched for a blue-eyed blonde with long legs. I was a simple small town girl, naive, ready to fall in love, and trusting — that is what men were and still are attracted to in me, despite the fact that I am almost forty."

"Fifty," I noted, barely audible.

"Yes, even though I am far on the north side of thirty, men still notice me. Every time I walk outside..."

I grabbed at the new opportunity: "Great. Let's test that."

"Do you not believe me?!" there was a threat to my peace in this question.

"Of course, I do! However, as President Reagan, a Russian proverb aficionado, used to say — trust but verify."

"Alright! Bet you as soon as I show up in the street, not a single man will ignore me."

"Let's verify!"

I suggested my wife stand on the corner of Brighton 5th Street and Oceanview Avenue in Brooklyn. On that corner, in the '80s and '90s, sat a house that was used as a secret brothel where local Russian-speaking immigrants used the services of Central American women.

My wife picked a suitable outfit — a low cut blouse, a short skirt, tall boots, and, for some reason, a wide-brimmed hat.

We drove to the agreed-upon spot. Once my wife positioned herself on the corner, I crossed the street to watch from a distance. We stood. We waited. Cars with lone men driving drove by without slowing. My wife pulled the collar of her blouse even lower. It had no effect. She pulled up the skirt higher. No result. On other corners of the same street plain Latin American women of middle age showed up every now and then; cars stopped, and, after a short negotiation, the woman took the passenger seat next to the driver. Watching my wife's gloomy face, I turned away so she did not see me shaking with laughter.

Eventually, a car stopped near her. At the wheel was... yours truly.

"The test is over. I am a poor pimp, and you are no woman of questionable social standards. Let's go home."

We both laughed the whole way home, only the shades of laughter were different for each of us. My laughter was victorious, and my wife's was awkward.

So, you think this adventure taught her something? You don't know my wife!

Desperately Searching
for a Prostitute

A t one time, in the late 1980s, the New York studio of Radio Liberty ran a daily broadcast called Broadway 1775. The title was, I believe, suggested by writer Sergei Dovlatov, and was the street address of the studio.

Every day the chief editor of the Russian language broadcast in New York Yuri Gendler gave out assignments to the reporters. And the unforgettable day came, when I, with my ill luck, was assigned to find on the streets of the city a woman of "low social responsibility" and interview her about the secrets and peculiarities of her trade. I set off with great enthusiasm.

In those days, prostitutes were easiest to find in the area of the Central Bus Station on 8th Avenue in West Side Manhattan where an entire city block was taken over by adult shops. I decided to cover the territory from 34th Street — from the Javits Center to the Bus Station on 42nd Street. I arrived at my starting point by subway and walked the street, glancing around for a woman that I imagined would be one of low moral standards. Just in case, I had the tape recorder ready.

Not a single obvious prostitute was to be seen. I must have looked like a hunter when I with borderline lust stared at every woman in my way, because all women picked up their pace. "My dear prostitutes," I thought, "where have you all gone?" Just then, instead of a prostitute, I suddenly ran into an old acquaintance from Moscow. a new immigrant in New York who was learning the layout of the city.

"Hello there!"

"Hi!"

"What are you up to?"

"Looking for prostitutes."

"Can I tag along?"

"Sure."

I figured he was a handsome guy and I could use him as bait for women.

So, we walked, talking about this and that and glancing around. No luck, not a single prostitute! It was the middle of the day. These night butterflies must only come out in the dark and now were resting after the previous night's labors. We reached the bus station. No prostitutes. Not one. It was as if someone had tipped them off about my hunt. And I had my deadline looming. It would be shameful and unprofessional not to fulfill the assignment. What could I do?

At a loss, I called my wife: "Honey, I haven't found any prostitutes, I'm heading your way." She responded: "Don't worry, I'll think of something. Come home."

I said goodbye to my friend and got on a subway train. Soon I was home in Brooklyn. My wife was waiting for me in the car. "Get in, let's go." "Where?" "Coney Island." For those who may not know, Coney Island is a high crime area of South Brooklyn, famous for its amusement park and low income apartment complexes. Back in the day, that area next to Brighton Beach was one of the most notorious in New York City. That's where my wife drove me in search of prostitutes. I have no idea how she knew where to find them, but we did not have to search for long.

We stopped by two dark-skinned girls, barely dressed, according to their occupation. "Hello!" I said with a Russian accent. "I am a reporter. I want to interview you. Anonymously. You don't have to give me your name." The girls looked at each other and then around. With no potential client in sight, they agreed to talk with me.

I pressed the "record" button.

"We agree, because we don't get reporters asking us questions nearly as often as cops."

They told me about different kinds of risks of their occupation, mostly health-related. Apart from that, it seemed to operate like any other business: serious competition, ratings, scheming, but good tax-free pay in cash.

I will not dwell on the details of the conversation. I will, however, share the girls' answer to one of my questions.

"Have you thought about changing jobs?"

"We have."

"What would you like to do?"

"Counseling, of course."

"Why?"

"We practice every day and have a lot of experience. We recognize the psychotype of a man as soon as we know his intentions. Believe me, prostitutes are the best psychologists."

I turned off the recording and said to my wife: 'Time to go!"

"Hold on," said one of the girls. "What about pay? We spent time on you when we could have made good money."

I always respected real professionals, so I fished out a bill out of my pocket and gave it to one of the girls. I got in the car. The second girl bent down and whispered in my ear: "Next time come without the wife."

My assignment was done.

A Cry of a Soul

Well, ladies, what shall we do about men?

The options are to change them or live without them. The first one is preferable: change them. Just look at them — those are not men but limp noodles.

During the War, naturally, there was a shortage of men at home. We women handled the factories, the harvest, and the livestock.

But the War was a long time ago. Yet we still live like it's wartime. Who is at the factory? A woman. Who is in the field? A woman. The home and the livestock is on her. What is on the men? Pants. But we wear pants too.

I have a friend who is three times dismarried. She says: "Enough. I can't see these roosters anymore. We women, the fools we are, wait for them — hello, thank you, finally you are here. Right. They fly into your coop, hang around and leave. And all you have left is to say — well, that was supposed to happen."

Another girlfriend of mine will not marry. She says: "I'd rather have a dog. A dog is your friend. A husband is your enemy. A dog whines when you're gone and wags its tail when you're back. A husband whines when you're there and wags his tail when you're not around. Of course, a dog sniffs at random mutts too, but you can walk him on a leash or even keep him on a chain. A husband, though? Try to put him on a chain and he turns into a beast! I'm telling you, a bulldog is better. What if its face is ugly? Are many men prettier? What if it has bowed legs? So does your man! A husband comes from work and stares into the TV and won't talk. I can bark back and forth with a bulldog! One four-legged guy is better than two two-legged ones!"

This friend of mine may be right, but... A bulldog is a bulldog. I want to meet a man! I want to meet a man so very much! A real man, strong and calm, masculine and kind, with the eyes I could drown in, an understanding smile, and a responsive heart. I don't need anything more. I would live for him. I would suffer for him. And he would carry me, and not I — him.

Where is he? Where have they all gone, our knights in shining armor?

I hear there used to be those knights — tall, broad shouldered, with great mustaches and greater courage. They would go to war for their lady. They did not spare their lives.

Now? No height, no shoulders, no... Well, some have mustaches. But what sort of mustaches are those? They just tickle you. Nowadays, they do not spare lives, either, but not their own — their women's. Women lay rails instead of table runners and asphalt instead of bedsheets. Look at our arms! Look at our shoulders! Some of us have learned to live without men at all. And what choice do we have? Okay, let's do a test: let him who thinks himself a real knight stand up!

Watch — not a single one. Ah, there, there is one... and another one. Bless their hearts! Really, have you ever heard of a knight who obeys a woman's command?

A Martian in Brighton Beach

Once an alien appeared in Brighton Beach; an oddball. He did not speak Russian. He did not understand Yiddish. He was strangely and poorly dressed — not fashionably, not in Italian brands. He walked and stared. People came out of the shops and stopped scrutinizing oranges, distracted by the alien; they surrounded him and asked where he was from. A few days before they saw a movie about Martians on TV. Someone wondered if this alien was also an extraterrestrial, E.T. for short. People used sign language to explain to him that this was Brighton; over there was the Primorsky restaurant; here, the Black Sea bookstore; and the whole place was known as Little Odessa of Brooklyn. He nodded, but clearly did not understand. He had to be a Martian if he didn't know Odessa! He looked like a human — one nose, two arms, two legs... People touched him to make sure everything was in order. He was just like a human, only very thin. There must be food shortages on Mars, and that is why he had come to Brighton.

There was such an abundance in Little Odessa that anyone's eyes would pop. A nice old woman took pity on him and bought him a meat pie. He ate it and visibly felt better. He smiled and all of a sudden said in a human voice: "Delicious!" The people stirred and were asking one another what the word meant. Someone remembered that "delicious" was the English word for a delicacy, something tasty. Oh, the alien was American! Go figure! He must have come there from as far as Manhattan!

For a long time yet, grandmothers told their grandchildren the tale of a real American in Brighton.

Everything is Wrong

You just came to America and you know nothing. You do everything wrong, not the way it's supposed to be done. You were born in a wrong place and married a wrong woman. You left at the wrong time and arrived at the wrong place. You rented the wrong apartment in the wrong part of town. You took lessons in the wrong language from the wrong tutor. You had the wrong things mailed to the wrong address. You took the wrong job for the wrong money.

You take the wrong subway train and go in the wrong direction.

You look the wrong way, hear the wrong things, you misunderstand and think the wrong thoughts.

You buy the wrong groceries in the wrong shops and not on sale.

You have the wrong friends; your gait is off.

You go to the wrong doctor — not the one who knows a lot and charges little.

Your accent is wrong and so are your jokes.

You are not at all what you seem to be and not at all who you say you are.

Everyone talks about it. Everyone says you do things wrong. Everyone says your way of doing things is wrong. They say it after the fact, after you have already done it.

And you? What can you say to them in your defense apart from that you have nothing to say to them? But even when you do not say anything, you do it wrong!

You do everything wrong, not the correct way.

Your only consolation is that you are not alone.

Heard It Through the Grapevine

"You have no idea! This guy told me that he easily got a permit for a machine gun. Yup. Just try to trespass on him now. He has four machine guns in four windows. He also put a small WWII howitzer in front of the door. And nobody can say anything. You know why? He showed them a form proving he is a weapons collector. It's a hobby. Now he's saving for a bomber.

"There's this other guy. You're not gonna believe it! Nobody believes it. Guess what job he got? He's doing very well now. You know what his job is? He bought a house with a pool, and that sports car, a Model 3000 convertible... And a young French woman comes to wash it every Saturday! That's the life! So, do you know what he does? He must have paid someone ten thousand for that spot, or even forty! He is a garbage collector! One Italian guy connected him through an Irishman. He's doing great now. The truck collects garbage, and he collects the money.

"You have no idea how people get by here! This guy told me about this other guy. He came here with nothing. He took florist classes and was making funeral wreaths. Now he is a doctor. Either a psychologist or a dietician. He tells people that stress is bad for them and vegetables are good. He charges a hundred dollars for a session. He has an office in Manhattan and two assistants, both Japanese women.

"I've been thinking. Next year I will become a citizen and have the right to vote. I think I'll join a political party. Who knows, I may be elected to Congress eventually. I will move to

D.C. and speak on TV. There I'll learn English whether I want it or not. Now, I have no motivation. What do I need English in Brighton Beach for? Nobody in their right mind speaks English here."

"Am I Right, Woman?!"

(Arguments of a husband who does not want to get off the couch)

Ok, I moved to New York City, found a job and an apartment, what's next?

Ok, I moved to New York City, left my job, started my own business, bought a house, divorced you, Manya, and what's next?

Ok, I moved to New York City, sold one business, bought another, bought two more houses and a condo in Florida, got a St.Bernard dog and another wife. What's next?

Ok, I moved to New York, made my first ten million, traveled the globe, bought a Rolls Royce, a yacht, a harbor, took Angelina Jolie as a lover, put a diamond ring in my nose. What's next?

Next I'm going to want to abandon it all to hell, hide from paparazzi in a hole somewhere in Detroit and enjoy a simple life as a regular American.

So I am asking you, Manya, do we have to move from Detroit to that damned New York City? Do we? No? That's exactly what I've been trying to tell you the whole time!

On the Beach

On a New York beach, a group of immigrants from Odessa is sunbathing. A heavy older woman leaves the group and combs the beach in search of entertainment. In her way is a man reading a newspaper in Russian. A cute dog lies next to the man. The woman reaches down to the dog.

"What a cutie pie! Look at those pretty eyes! Mister, is this your dog?"

"Mine", the man replies, still reading.

"What a handsome dog! As handsome as Alain Delon! I'd name him Alaindelon. What about you?"

"I'd name him Buster, if he wasn't already named Buddy."

"Oh... What is *your* name, then?"

"Igor."

"Really? The name suits you. And you have such a cute doggie!.. Do you work?"

"I work."

"What's your job?"

"I'm a milling operator."

"A real milling operator?! Misha!" She yells across the beach to someone in her group. "Misha, come here! Meet Igor. He is the man we need!"

Her group does not stir, baking their round bellies in the sun.

"Say, what part of town do you work in?"

"Canarsie."

"Misha! Don't move! This is not what we need! It's too far!.. How much do you make?"

"Much."

"Misha! Stop lying about and come here, quick!.. Are you in a union?"

"No union."

"Misha! Don't move!.. Sorry, that's not what we need."

And she continues on in search of the next victim of her profit-seeking curiosity.

A Monologue
of a Lady Who Looks Her Age

"Well, have you heard anything new? Yes, yes. At our age, it is hard to hear anything. Have you been to the doctor? Why not? Have you not received Medicaid yet? What are they thinking? People are suffering. Oh how we suffered! We waited for our things to arrive for five months. It turned out they got lost! And it wasn't a tiny powder box, either, pardon me. That was nine containers, half a tonne each! They lost them! They lost them, and I have a weak heart! Well, they found them. But at what cost to me! I won't even mention how much stuff was missing and who might have needed a single candelabra piece, two table legs, and three slippers. Was he a freak with three feet? And what do you think of this organization that is supposed to help us? All they want is to push you out to work, the sooner the better. They should be supporting a person for a year or two, providing for them, teaching them the language and a trade. Giving them a good start...

But no. They just kick you out to work! I'm not a simple girl, though. I said, alright, give me a job I am qualified for. My specialty is managing a warehouse. Give me a warehouse, and I'll manage it, I told them. Do you know what job they offered me? A waitress! A waitress, with my aching feet! Still, I said, okay, good. They gave me an address. They said it was a private club, invited guests only. Okay, I went there. It was in the middle of Manhattan. The door and the walls were covered in tiny mirrors, like fish scales. I opened the door... to see barely dressed women! I understood immediately it was a brothel. Did I leave my old brothel to end up in theirs? Of course, I understand it was not intentional. They saw an ad that said waitresses were needed, so they sent me there. I'd send them there myself! There, and on from there! If I am such a bother, why did they invite me? What do you mean, nobody invited me? I listened every night to their Voice of America saying how good it was in America and how bad it was in Russia. Did they say that? They did. Had they said it the other way round, I'd never have come. Had they said that it was bad in America and good in Russia, I'd have stayed put, because I'd have known that others had it even worse. So, they invited me. Now I'm their problem."

Yasha the Lucky

"Have you heard?"

"What's up?"

"Have you heard what luck Yasha has had?"

"Which Yasha? He of 10 Pushkin Street?"

"No, he of 11 Lenin Street."

"Well, what happened to him?"

"He has had such luck that you wish God would give it to us and our children!"

"Well, what is it?!"

"Will you let me speak?"

"Okay, I'll be quiet. Well?"

"I tell you, he struck gold! This is how it went. He just came to America and learned that newcomers can have free healthcare for a while. And, go figure, he had no complaints — nothing hurt! You know our people's luck: when we can have, we don't need, and when we need, we can't have. Now, he was told that the most expensive were eyes and teeth. And Yasha can do math. He did some math and realized that thirty-two teeth would cost him more than two eyes. So, he decided, before it was too late, to lose a tooth. A tooth is not an eye, one doesn't need it that bad, unless one wants to crack nuts. At the moment it was free, and later it would be cheaper. If Yasha sets out to do something, he will do it. When he decided to marry a girl from Kherson, he went to Kherson, and nobody could stop him! Of course, nobody thought about stopping him... Nobody cared. Anyway, that's not the point. The point is, he went to a dentist. The dentist took a look and said that Yasha's teeth were like tile in a Hollywood star's bathroom. Yasha, for some reason, got upset, and asked the dentist to pull a tooth. The dentist refused. Yasha insisted. An argument started. Well, you know Yasha, he can't keep his hands to himself. It turned out, the dentist couldn't, either. So, Yasha got lucky. He was sitting in the chair with that dental machine hanging over him. The dentist stood next to it. The dentist was agitated and waving his arms. So, he hit the machine and it tipped over and fell on Yasha's head. Mind you, that machine is made of metal."

"What a misfortune!"

"You mean, what fortune! Yes, a fortune of forty kilograms fell on Yasha's head. Or even fifty. Now, for the injury and the emotional damage, he got such a huge payoff and also such a permanent disability check that he does not have to work ever again and his family is provided for. Fancy that! I saw him recently. He dresses like the husband of a beauty salon owner. He wears rings on everything he can put a ring on. He looks at people as if he's searching for someone to give a million dollars to. Of course, he now stammers a little, twitches a little, and has some minor mental issues. But that is so trivial compared to how happy he is!"

"Some people are so lucky! My husband has a twitch also, but nobody pays him for it."

"That's a different matter! Your husband brought his twitch to America, so why does America have to pay for an immigrant twitch? It's different in Yasha's case. Yasha did a good job! Yasha is smart! Yasha is lucky!"

How to Spend Money

Money is best spent when there's a lot of it. The more money, the better. The most pointless expenditure is on your spouse. The most common sense is to spend on yourself.

One can spend cleverly. One can spend mindlessly. One spends mindlessly, when buying everything at random believing that tomorrow it will be more expensive. One spends cleverly, when not buying anything believing that tomorrow it will be cheaper.

One must part with money easily and with good humor. To that end, we recommend responding to the following advertisement:

"Language skills not required! Any age! Work from home! Would you like to make $150 per day? Send us only $10 and we will teach you how!"

Done? Now, you wait. You may get the following response: "Thank you for the $10. You have begun learning. Send us $15 and we will mail you the instructions."

Most finish their learning at this point. But, if you are a curious type, send the $15 and you will most certainly receive the following response: "Congratulations on your achievement! We have mailed you the instructions. However, the instructions are not sufficient by themselves. Send us only $43 and we will mail you the textbooks."

As you see, the course of study can be ongoing. Still, the effect is obvious: you have learned to part with your money easily and with good humor.

How to Talk to Americans

I f you are a new immigrant in America and your English is far from adequate, for starters it is enough to learn just nine words and phrases that will help you pass for a local when talking to an American.

For example, you are in the subway and an outgoing American comes up to you and says something angrily. Of course, it would be only natural to let him know that you have just recently moved to the country and are still incompetent in both local issues and the local tongue. But that is not how we roll! If we do not know something, we never admit to it, especially to a stranger. Meanwhile, the American continues in his frustration. He may be upset with inflation or his wife. In this case, we recommend alternating nodding and smiling sympathetically with the phrase: "Take it easy!" which corresponds to the Russian "don't take it in your head." After these words, the American will either calm down and shut up, or get even more frustrated and will keep talking for so long that you will not have to respond anyway. Mission accomplished.

"Delicious" goes well with turkey and mushrooms or tea and crackers when visiting someone's home.

"Fantastic" is another good one. This word can express feelings ranging from surprise to awe. Americans tend to be awed by very insignificant things. By using the word "fantastic" you can pass for a native of southwestern Brooklyn.

If you strive to appear 100% American, learn to say "Beautiful!" It is a wonderful word and will accompany you in America like a tiny dog following an old lady. American women, especially those whose age is determined by the number of fake flowers on their hats, believe that the beautiful word "beautiful" and the admiration expressed by it helps one live longer.

In general, America cultivates positive emotions. Just as in the old country we used to say: "Take a rest, Vanya!" here they say"Relax!" and "Don't worry!".

Now learn "Hi", "Bye", and "Okay" and you will be ready to bravely sail the sea of American people.

How to Marry

Marry, if you really have to. But do it wisely.

How? Never take advice from amateurs. In this delicate matter, only a professional can give an exhaustive answer.

Through studying of marriage ads, polling of your mates, and utilizing the experience of the previous victims of the marriage scheme, one can come to the following conclusions.

Some prospective grooms prefer lady immigrants from Moscow, others — from Odessa, yet others do not have a preference.

One can marry for love... of the bride's money. One can marry for profit... and fall in love with his wife later.

Marriages can be happy and unhappy, premature, late, or what they call misalliances.

A happy marriage can be described this way: "They lived happily ever after and died on the same day". This usually happens in fairy tales.

An unhappy marriage is when two people live together for a long time out of spite and compete in who outlives the other. This sometimes happens in real life.

A premature marriage is when he says he is too young to marry, and his family still makes him do it.

A late marriage is when she says that he is too old to marry, but he, due to his age, does not realize it.

A misalliance is when she is tall and he is short; she is thin and he is fat; she is dark-haired and he is bald.

A bride can come with or without a dowry. The dowry may contain jewelry, savings, real estate, or an even more real mother-in-law.

A bride without a dowry is usually a pure charming creature with a little brat in tow.

It is customary for the bride to wear white, for the groom to wear black, for the mother of the bride to wear tears, and for the toastmaster to wear salad.

One can marry a classmate, a colleague, or a mistress.

Professionals recommend marrying the latter. A mistress turned wife will provide the assurance of loyalty to your wife and a false feeling of freedom.

How to Give Advice

Americans love to give advice. It is free and, at the same time, gives one the satisfaction of having done a good deed of helping your neighbor.

Say you are a new immigrant. You came here, found a cheap apartment, but ran out of money and can't afford a bed. You go to a second cousin in the hope to borrow some cash from her. The cousin greets you cheerfully and excitedly: "Welcome, my dear!"

You have had tea, and now you carefully start telling your story. You tell her you are doing great, but lack some basic furniture. The cousin immediately springs into action. She advises against buying cheap furniture — it is of bad quality and will fall apart within a year. She recommends an expensive and reputable furniture store. She even makes a phone call and finds out the name of the best store in New York City.

Exhausted by this effort and pleased with herself, she invites you to come visit anytime and let her know if you need anything — she is always happy to help. "And do not do anything without consulting me first!"

She stands up. You stand up. You kiss the air by each other's cheeks and say tearful goodbyes.

How to Cheer Someone Up

How are you? Are you whining again? Want me to cheer you up? You think I can't? Try me!

What's up? Why are you complaining again? Is life hard? Who has it easy? You don't have enough? Who does? They? You think they have enough? Your health isn't that good? And whose is? Theirs? How do you know? Are you a doctor? You don't love your wife? Who does? He does? You think he loves his wife? Someone else's wife, likely. Do you think loving someone else's wife is easy? Are you sure? So, if someone else's wife becomes yours and yours becomes someone else's, will you love your ex more because she belongs to another guy now? Maybe just pretend yours isn't yours to begin with?

What is it? Nobody understands you? Who do you think they understand? That one? Or them over there? Do they even understand themselves? Do they understand anything at all?

You don't like your place? Who does? Do you think they do? Do you think they would like to ride a bus for an hour, walk for another half hour, climb the stairs to the fourth floor and share their home with a family of cockroaches?

What's wrong with the roaches? Do they drink vodka and scream at the top of their lungs all night? Do they insult you? Do they ask you for money to treat their hangover?

Are you so picky that mice annoy you also? You are not? Then what are you complaining about?

What? You can't afford a car? You don't have a driver's license? Who does? He does? They do? Did you have a license *back there*? What is a Jew licensed to do *back there* in the first place? To bribe? In exchange for what? What is left *back there* that is Jewish, except for the graveyard? Wasn't the graveyard the only place where a Jew wasn't ashamed to be a Jew? Wasn't it the only place Jews were allowed to enter? Why were you happy *back there*? Why are you unhappy here?

What? You are lonely? You are lonely *here*? Were you not lonely *back there*? Were we all not lonely *back there*? If you call out "hello!" back there, will you hear a human response or only barking of guard dogs?

You are not valued? People like you are a dime a dozen here. Do you think they don't know your worth? Do you think they will sacrifice to make you happy? Haven't they already done it? Did they need you or did you need them? Was their business at a standstill before you arrived? Was their birth rate low? Did they lack Russian teachers with an Odessa accent?

What are you whining about? Are you a genius? A prodigy? Do you have two noses? Do you have money? Does your wife love you? Do you not live with roaches? Does your mind produce something more than scrambled eggs?

Do you want to have everything right away? You want everything you had there on top of everything they have here? What are you doing to get that? You whine.

Stop whining! You don't have any friends? How about enemies? Is it boring without any enemies? I can be your enemy! Want me to prove that I'm a lousy friend but a priceless enemy? What? Are you smiling? And you didn't believe that I could cheer you up. You didn't believe I wanted to help you. You thought you were alone, friendless, and unwanted. What about me?

So, why were you whining? Are you not a good looking guy? What about those eagle eyes and an eagle nose? Aren't you an expert at what you do? Aren't you handy? Isn't your head a virtual library?

Enough whining. Stop ruining your own mood. Step away from the mirror, go work out, brush your teeth and get to work. Well? Go!

"That's my boy," I said to my reflection in the mirror.

How to Handle a Man

I have read that marriage is unstable nowadays. As for me, ladies, I think it is our own fault. We're doing it wrong. For example, if I'm going to acquire a refrigerator or a vacuum cleaner I have plenty of options: I can make payments, I can lease one, or I can pay cash. I also get a warranty and an owner's manual.

But, let's say I wanted to make payments on a husband. I'd collect all sorts of proof of good credit history and good references. I'd pre-order a husband. Then I'd make payments with every paycheck for five years. Would I ever leave him then? Never! I'd take the best care of the dear man and wouldn't let him out of my sight! I'd know if I mistreated him, he would break. Then I'd have hell to go through to have him fixed.

Now, say, he had a fault. Say, he drank too much or something. I'd call tech support and tell them. They would say they didn't have the correct parts, the production line had stopped, and the foreign machines kept breaking... or some such. What then?

"Then," I would say, "replace the whole works!"

"We can't," they would say. "The unit is damaged due to mishandling by the owner. You violated the warranty. You have to throw this one away and purchase a new one."

To avoid such a horrible situation, I would much rather memorize all the rules and hang posters of them on the walls instead of paintings. To the right will be "recommendations", to the left — "a brief description", behind — "technical characteristics", and in front — "operation MANual".

Here is what the Operation MANual will say:

"Attention! Before purchasing Unit MAN 1.0 request to check its correct operation. Make sure all the seals are intact and all the parts are present. Before plugging the unit in, make sure that the voltage in your house matches that of the unit. Read the Owner's MANual; learn the controls and external connection locations. Do not leave the operating unit unattended."

"Technical characteristics": Unit MAN 1.0 of average size, average fuel capacity, average speed, and average excitability complies with the average international standards and is meant to be used at home as well as outside. The unit retains its function up to the internal temperature of 40 Celcius. Must be regularly powered down. Weight without accessories does not exceed 150 kilograms.

"Brief description": The body of the unit consists of three parts: top, middle, and bottom. The top part is attached to the bottom part by the middle part. When powered on, the unit begins to function.

"Operation MANual": Keep Unit MAN 1.0 clean. Regularly wipe with a soft cloth soaked in rubbing alcohol. Keep at the temperature of 36.6 Celsius. Do not apply dangerous chemicals. Keep fuelled. Dust thoroughly. Do not provoke the unit to anger. Do not mock. Do not intrude on private thoughts — death or injury may occur. Regularly add lubricant. Keep in a warm, dry place. To avoid bursting, do not punch.

If these instructions are not followed, Unit MAN 1.0 may explode. If the instructions are followed, we guarantee normal operation for a year after purchase."

I think that if the instructions are followed, he will operate normally for a hundred years.

A Piece of Advice for Married Men

If your wife says that she's going on a business trip, why wouldn't you believe that she is actually going on a business trip?

If your wife, after a long day at work, does not want to eat the leftover soup you cooked the night before and says that her friend's husband cooks fresh every day, do not get angry, do not pout, and by no means cry. Women do not like crying men. Crying men annoy them. Ask for that friend's phone number, get hold of her husband, and ask him to share recipes with you. The man may turn out to be a cool guy and you may be able to hang out and chat about the hard life of a man while your wives are at work.

If your wife does not return home at the usual time, do not call her workplace or her friends or police. This can make her a laughing stock for her colleagues. Consider the possibilities: she may have had to stay late at work; she may have gone to a bar after for a beer or two with a friend; then they may have gone to visit another friend for a round of poker — this can take as long as four hours. After a hard day at work, beer, and poker, she could have spent the night on a friend's couch and gone to work the next day from there. If your wife returns home after a month — you were right, everything is okay, and there was no need to worry. This new gray hair of yours is just a sign of age.

If you are walking down the street and a strange woman catches up with you and says: "I know you from somewhere! Have you been starred in a movie?" — she is obviously hitting on you. You can easily tell what her intentions are. If you are not inclined to encourage her, say something disarming and original, like "I do not flirt with strange women in the street" or "By the way, I am married and my wife happens to be a wrestling champion."

If you cannot get your wife pregnant, do not blame yourself. It can lead to low self esteem. In this day and age, there are plenty of ways to achieve this goal.

The way a man looks plays an important role in his life. If your wife always sees you in the same set of PJs and slippers, and if, upon waking up, she sees you groggy and ungroomed, how long will she put up with you? Every morning you must rise before her, make yourself presentable, make coffee and be ready for her to wake. Do not grumble if, as a result, she feels desire, and you have to undress and then dress again and make coffee one more time. In the end, isn't this what we live for?

Even if you are happy in your marriage, we do not recommend you live only through your wife's interests. You are entitled to your own private life, your little secrets, and your small manly tricks.

If your wife comes home from work and plops on the couch with a newspaper or stares at the TV, do not bother her by saying that you have waited all day to talk with her and to share the news and that she must not love you at all and that, if things do not change, you will pack your stuff and go live with your dad. Do not say any of that. Pick up a calming occupation: knitting, dusting furniture, or reading advice for married men. It is very important not to disturb your wife with your presence. When she wishes to see you, she will call for you. She has to see in you the meek desire to obey. After all, she, as the breadwinner and the head of the household, has every right to it.

To avoid domestic conflict, carve on a stone tablet or embroider on your favorite pillow that you cry into at night the following: your wife is always right, even when she is wrong.

M.Mann, Doctor of Manology

Good and Bad

It was bad there, so we left and came to where it was good. It turned out that where it is good, it is not good all the time — sometimes it is bad. And where it was bad, they say it is good now. So, it is bad where we are and good where we are not. I have been thinking. Why do some have it good and some have it bad? Why don't we all go to where it is good now to make it bad there and to make it good here where it is sometimes bad? It is good that it will be bad there, but then we will be where it is bad; that means it will be bad for us. Why would we make it bad for ourselves? It's better to make it even better where it's not that bad. Because when something is good, everything is good, and when something is bad, everything is bad. It's better when it's good. On the other hand, everything can't be good; something always has to be bad. Then let it be bad; but not all the way, only halfway bad. Halfway bad and the other half very good! And that halfway point has to be at the end when it doesn't matter all that much anymore if it is good or bad. When it makes no difference — good or bad. When it can't be good. When it's only bad. And after that, good!

Let's Show It to Someone for a Second Opinion

A Playlet

Cast of Character's:

Raisa: an elderly woman, sister of Alexandra
Alexandra: an elderly woman, sister of Raisa

SETTING: A large room with expensive antique furniture:
a Wardrobe, a sofa, a mirror in an elaborate frame.
To the left is a grand piano. In the back is an easel.
Behind the easel — a large window. To the right are two arm-
chairs. In the armchairs lounge two white-haired women. The
shorter one Raisa is knitting.
The taller one Alexandra is reclining and dozing.
Raisa is quietly singing Jules Massenet's Elegie.
Alexandra with her eyes still closed, starts singing along.

RAISA *(clicking the knitting needles)*: It will be done in three
days or so.
ALEXANDRA: What are you knitting?
RAISA: I've told you, a case.
ALEXANDRA: Ah, yes, so you have. A case for what?
RAISA: I don't know yet.

*(RAISA resumes singing. ALEXANDRA opens her eyes and
watches RAISA knit.)*

ALEXANDRA: It's pretty.
RAISA: Do you really like it? I'll give it to you when it's done.
ALEXANDRA: Thank you.

RAISA: It's time for your medicine.
ALEXANDRA: Not yet. I'm so warm here.

(RAISA adjusts her throw.)

RAISA: I like it warm too, and the fireplace... Do you re-member?

(RAISA recites)

> "The coals are burning out and in the dark
> A fragile flame is dancing
> Like a butterfly with azure wings
> Flutters on a crimson poppy flower.
> A caravan of colorful images
> Is a sight for sore eyes.
> And mysterious faces
> Look out from the ashes of the fireplace."

Good, isn't it?
ALEXANDRA: I am not a fan of Afanasy Fet.
RAISA: He is better than what they write nowadays, in any case.
ALEXANDRA: Yes, of course.

(RAISA puts away her knitting)

RAISA: That's enough for today.
ALEXANDRA: What are you going to do now?
RAISA: I do not know.

(Pause)

RAISA: Read out of Thomas Chatterton to me.
ALEXANDRA: I don't feel like it.

(Pause)

RAISA: I'll go work on my painting.

(RAISA goes to the easel, picks up brushes and a palette, makes a few strokes.)

RAISA: I would like to finish it today. I think this time I can do it.

ALEXANDRA: Don't ever say it before you actually finish it.

RAISA: Ah, but I am not superstitious.

(ALEXANDRA laughs)

ALEXANDRA: Of course you are not!

(RAISA steps away from the easel and looks at the painting)

RAISA: I need your advice. I thought of adding a few more details... to define it... and for the mood... but I'm afraid to ruin it. Maybe I should just leave alone...

ALEXANDRA: Let me see.

(RAISA turns the easel.)

ALEXANDRA: It's good. Don't add anything.

(RAISA smiles, happy.)

RAISA: I am so glad! To be honest, I was afraid that you wouldn't like it.

ALEXANDRA: It would be good if someone else took a look, for a second opinion.

RAISA: I think Rubb was going to stop by today.

ALEXANDRA: Who?

RAISA: Mr.Rubb. He is a rich patron of modern art. He was going to stop by at two o'clock.

ALEXANDRA: It is already half past.

RAISA: He must be on his way.

(RAISA goes to the window, looks out, walks away.)

RAISA: I think I heard a knock.

ALEXANDRA: You imagined it.

RAISA: I must have.

(Pause)

RAISA: Tell me something.

ALEXANDRA: What?

RAISA: I don't know.
ALEXANDRA: Me, neither.

(RAISA goes to the piano and lightly touches the keys.)

ALEXANDRA: Push me close.

(RAISA pushes ALEXANDRA in her chair to the piano. ALEX-
ANDRA begins to play. RAISA listens to the wonderful sounds
brought out of the instrument by a master. ALEXANDRA sudden-
ly stops playing and puts her hands on her knees.)

RAISA: Bravo! Bravo!
ALEXANDRA: Quiet!
RAISA: What is it?
ALEXANDRA: Do you hear?
RAISA: Hear what?
ALEXANDRA: Applause, somewhere... Yes, they are ap-
plauding! Don't you hear?

(RAISA pretends to hear.)

RAISA: They truly are!
ALEXANDRA: Are they out in the street? Take a look.
RAISA: They must be.

(RAISA goes to the window.)

RAISA: Nobody in the street.
ALEXANDRA: How about outside the front door?

(RAISA opens the door.)

RAISA: Nobody here.
ALEXANDRA: I must have imagined it.
RAISA: You must have.
ALEXANDRA: Take me back to my spot.

(RAISA pushes ALEXANDRA to her usual spot. A pause.)

ALEXANDRA: I am sad. Talk to me.
RAISA *(with enthusiasm)*: What about?
(Pause.)

ALEXANDRA: Nevermind. Everything has already been said.

(RAISA agrees with the same enthusiasm.)

RAISA: Yes, everything has been said... You know, I think I'll move this table over there. We can set the flower pot from the window on it.

ALEXANDRA: Why not?

(RAISA moves the table and the flower.)

RAISA: Well, what do you think?

ALEXANDRA: Not bad for a change.

RAISA: The flower looks good here. By the way, yesterday I wrote a poem about flowers.

ALEXANDRA: Did you really?

RAISA: Would you like to hear it?

ALEXANDRA: Of course!

RAISA: A Girl and a Daisy.

"In a field, there lived a daisy. It was very pretty: young, yellow-eyed, in a white dress. She looked like a ballet dancer magically frozen in the middle of a pirouette. Her neighbor, a dandelion, adored her, and the poppy spread his scarlet petals before her and considered proposing marriage. Suddenly, a girl ran into the field, picked the daisy and skipped away. The daisy was left on the ground, her petals gone, naked. Her yellow head drooped, her stalk was broken and crumpled. Her wilting petals were scattered around her and trembled in the wind. The daisy was cold and embarrassed. After a while, everyone forgot her. Only the old dandelion sighed sometimes, recalling her beauty. Eventually, he also forgot in the midst of his daily cares... The poppy married someone else the next day. He married a pansy. She wasn't as flashy as the daisy, but still attractive. She had beautiful eyes. And... nobody would use her to find out if 'he loves me, he loves me not'. Would you like to know the girl's fate? It was the same as that of the daisy."

ALEXANDRA: Good job. Wonderful.

(RAISA is embarrassed by such high praise.)

RAISA: You really like it?

ALEXANDRA: I wouldn't lie, would I? It is very well written. In good taste, with good rhythm, well-composed, clever, poetic, and vivid.

RAISA *(in a whisper)*: Thank you!

ALEXANDRA: You should send it to a magazine.

RAISA *(hopeful)*: You think it may be accepted?

ALEXANDRA: Why not?

RAISA: Well, they could say "We don't need this in such difficult times... The reader wants something entirely different..." They said that once, remember?

ALEXANDRA: It was years ago... However... Who knows... At least save it.

RAISA: Alright. It's time for your medication.

ALEXANDRA: This time you are correct.

(RAISA takes out a tiny bottle and a tiny glass, puts a few drops from the bottle into the glass, adds water, and hands the glass to ALEXANDRA. ALEXANDRA accepts the glass. Her hand shakes slightly, and she spills a bit of the liquid on the way to her mouth. ALEXANDRA drinks.)

RAISA: I spilled a bit. Wipe it, please.

(RAISA searches for something to wipe with, finds nothing. RAISA takes the paper with her poem, dabs at the wet spot, and tosses the crumpled wet paper into the trash basket.)

RAISA: Here you go. It's done. May I lie down? My feet ache. Do you mind?

ALEXANDRA: You don't have to ask! Of course, go lie down. You must take care of yourself. You must paint and write poetry. Maybe someday someone will need it all.

RAISA: Yes, of course, you are right.

(Passing by the easel, RAISA takes the painting off it, throws it behind the wardrobe and exits. ALEXANDRA is alone. She struggles to drag her chair to the piano and quietly plays Massenet's Elegie.)

Oh days of love, where have you gone,
Dreams so sweet,
Young dreams of spring?
Oh the forests full of birds sing,
Where are the flowers,
Moonlight and dawn?

O, doux printemps d'autre fois,
vertes saisons,
Vous avez fui pour toujours!
Je ne vois plus le ciel bleu;
Je n'entends plus
les chants joyeux des oiseaux!

(THE END. CURTAIN)

The Log

A One-Act Play

Cast of Characters:

WOMAN
MAN
YOUNG WOMAN
TWO FIGURES WITH A SUITCASE

SETTING: A room. From the back wall, a long and thick log protrudes and reaches the center of the living space.

Scene 1

(WOMAN aimlessly moves things around. The log is in her way. Every now and then, she bumps into it. WOMAN is tired, but does not give up. A fit MAN in high boots and an overcoat enters.)

MAN: Good evening.
WOMAN *(indifferently)*: Hello.
MAN: Hellish weather. I'm drenched. I'll leave as soon as I get warm, don't worry.

(WOMAN continues moving her things.)

WOMAN: Stay as long as you need. You are not bothering me. The more the merrier.

(MAN watches her work.)

MAN: Isn't the master of the house a merry fellow?

WOMAN: I am widowed. He died two years after we were married.

MAN: I see.

(Pause. MAN watches WOMAN work.)

MAN: Do you need a hand?

WOMAN: No, I've got it.

MAN: As you wish.

(WOMAN takes the overcoat off the chair back and tries to put it on a coat hook. Fails.
WOMAN moves the coat rack to the right and the chair with the overcoat to the left. WOMAN repeats this action several times.)

MAN: Let me...

(MAN takes the overcoat to the coat rack and hangs it.)

WOMAN *(surprised)*: Thank you. How did you do that?

MAN *(also surprised)*: I'm not sure... I must have thought about it a lot...

WOMAN *(missing the sarcasm)*: You must have. I am always so busy that I have no time to sit down, let alone to think. Well, what am I doing standing around? Let me finish this and I'll get you something to eat.

MAN: That would be great. I am so hungry that I can't bring myself to be polite and say "thank you, but I already ate".

(MAN closely watches her handling a bucket.)

MAN: But first, I would like some water.

WOMAN: In a moment... How do I do that, though?..

MAN: How about you bring the mug to the bucket instead of moving the bucket?.. There you are. And the radio can go over here.

(MAN puts the radio on the chair.)

MAN: This chair can stay here. And the mirror too. What do you think?

WOMAN *(truly astonished)*: You did in a minute what would have taken me my whole life! I fail to understand how... *(with emotion)* Thank you!

(WOMAN leaves to lay the table.)

MAN *(unmoving)*: Strange. Very strange.

(WOMAN returns.)

MAN: Is there somewhere I can wash my hands?
WOMAN: Through this door. The towel is there... Hold on...

(WOMAN takes a towel from the dresser drawer.)

WOMAN: Here it is.

(MAN accepts the towel, turns to the door and bumps into the log.)

MAN: Damn it!

(MAN leaves. WOMAN takes table linens out of the dresser. MAN returns and again hits the log.)

MAN: What the hell is this thing here for?

(WOMAN gives no response.)

MAN: Doesn't it get in your way?
WOMAN: Not at all. I'm used to it.
MAN: So it used to bother you?
WOMAN: A little. But that's the way it's supposed to be.
MAN: How do you figure?
WOMAN: Everyone has to be bothered by something. It is a necessity of life.
MAN: Why?
WOMAN *(drained)*: I don't know. They say so.

(WOMAN leaves.)

MAN: Very curious.

(MAN goes to the log and tries to budge it. WOMAN enters, runs to the man and pushes him away from the log.)

WOMAN: Don't you dare!
MAN: But it's in your way!
WOMAN: So?!
MAN: It must be removed. Cut off.
WOMAN: You can't cut off everything that's in your way.
MAN *(calmly)*: Makes sense.

(WOMAN points at the door to the next room.)

WOMAN: I made food for you.

(MAN exits. WOMAN slowly approaches the log and, as if seeing it for the first time, stares at it and warily touches it. MAN enters.)

MAN: Thank you for the food. *(Pause.)* I'd better be going.

(Pause. MAN picks up his coat.)

WOMAN: Stay. Live here for a while. You can always leave if you don't like it.

Scene 2

(Two days later. The stage setting has not changed, except for an added chair. WOMAN sits at the table, hemming a curtain. MAN sits next to her and watches her work. WOMAN pricks her finger.)

WOMAN: Ouch!
MAN: Are you hurt?
WOMAN: Yes. It's because you're watching me.
MAN: I like to watch someone work.
WOMAN: It can be unsettling.

(MAN stands up and crosses the room to the log.)

WOMAN *(urgently)*: Has it stopped raining?
MAN *(looking at the log)*: I think so.
WOMAN: No, it's still pouring.

(MAN does not respond.)

WOMAN: Will you look and see?

(MAN goes to the window.)

MAN: It's stopped.
WOMAN: That's good.

(MAN stares at the log again.)

WOMAN: Could you put a couple of nails in the wall for the curtain?
MAN: Where are the nails?
WOMAN: In the kitchen, with the tools.
MAN: And the hammer?
WOMAN: Same place.

(MAN exits. WOMAN looks at the log, gets up and walks to it. MAN enters with a hammer and nails. WOMAN quickly moves to the window.)
(MAN puts a nail to the wall.)

MAN: Is this okay? Higher?
WOMAN: No. Actually, a bit lower.
MAN: Here?
WOMAN: Yes.

(MAN hammers in two nails. WOMAN hangs the curtain. MAN, looking at the curtain, steps away backwards and again hits the log.)

MAN: Damn it! Someday I'll crack my skull on this stupid thing!

(WOMAN continues to adjust the curtain.)

MAN: Are you listening?!
WOMAN: I am.
MAN: Well, say something!
WOMAN: You'll get used to it.
MAN: You sure?
WOMAN: Yes.
MAN *(warily)*: Did everyone else?

WOMAN: Everyone.
MAN: Whoa!

(MAN nervously paces the room; stops.)

MAN: Who is "everyone"?

(WOMAN notices a hint of jealousy in MAN's voice and smiles.)

WOMAN: "Everyone" is my great-grandfather, my grandfather, my grandmother, my parents, my siblings, and I.
MAN: And your husband?
WOMAN *(after a pause)*: He would have.
MAN *(masking wariness with sarcasm)*: Didn't he have enough time?
WOMAN: After we got married, we lived with his family. I only returned here when he died.
MAN: Why did you return?
WOMAN: My parents wanted me around and didn't want the house to be empty after they were gone.
MAN: "Didn't want the house to be empty"... Your folks may have been right.

(MAN goes to the window.)

MAN: It's started raining again.
WOMAN: We should close the shutters, or the wind won't let us sleep.

(MAN turns to the door and runs into the log again.)

MAN *(outraged)*: I'm going to pull it out of the wall!
WOMAN: No! Please, don't. I am afraid.
MAN: What are you afraid of?!
WOMAN: I'm afraid the house will collapse.
MAN: This log isn't supporting anything. If it went from floor to ceiling, like a post, then sure. If it sat in the wall lengthwise and I were to knock it out, it would leave a huge gap. But it just sticks out of the wall for no reason. It doesn't bear any load and is good for nothing. We'll be perfectly fine without it!

WOMAN: What if the house falls down?!

MAN: It won't. I'll cut off part of it, right here. It will stay in the wall, but won't be sticking out into the room.

WOMAN: But what if the house still falls down?

MAN: It will not! How can it? How? Come here. Look, it is already loose. We'll be much better off without this log.

WOMAN: But what if the house falls down?

MAN: But why? Why would it fall down?! Here...

(MAN knocks on the log.)

MAN: Listen. It's a piece of wood, old, rotted wood that needs to go...

(MAN grabs the hammer).

WOMAN: No!

(WOMAN runs up to the man and embraces him.)

WOMAN: Please, I beg you, for the love of everything holy, don't do it!

(MAN drops the hammer, goes to the coat rack and puts on his coat.)

WOMAN *(voice strangled with fear)*: Where?..

(MAN goes to the door and responds after a pause.)

MAN: I'll go close the shutters.

Scene 3

(It's night. Sound of rain and howling of wind can be heard. Someone lights a match. Candlelight falls on MAN. MAN sets the candle on the table and goes to the log. MAN stares at it, grabs it and pulls. The log won't budge. MAN goes and gets the hammer. Hits the log. The sound is too loud. MAN puts the hammer away, grabs the log again and tries to get it loose. MAN pulls, and the log finally gives and slowly comes out of the wall. Once it's out, it leaves a hole in the wall. MAN carefully sets the log on the floor, fetches a round piece of fire-wood, plugs the hole, and, exhausted, sits on a chair. MAN listens and watches the log closely.)

MAN: There. The house still stands.

(MAN smiles and gets up. The smile slowly creeps off his face. Suddenly, MAN pulls out the chunk of firewood, picks up the log and carefully reinserts it into the wall. MAN checks if the log fits snugly. MAN picks up the firewood, goes to put it back in the corner and on his way back bumps into the log, hard.)

MAN: Ahhhh damn it!

(WOMAN comes running.)

WOMAN: What's wrong?
MAN: Nothing. I'm getting used to it.

Scene 4

(Twenty years have passed. The stage is the same, only one of the chairs is gone. On the windowsill sits a photograph of WOMAN in a black frame. MAN enters. He is older and his hair is white. MAN goes to the photo, looks at it for a long time, walks away, gazes around the room. Something bothers him. MAN goes to the coat rack with the intention to move it. He searches for a better spot. He picks up the coat rack, holds it for a moment, and sets it back down; walks off. There's a knock on the door. MAN goes to the window, looks out, sees the darkness and hears the rain. MAN goes to the door, skirting around the log with habitual ease. MAN opens the door. A YOUNG WOMAN of about twenty enters. YOUNG WOMAN is wearing a wet coat and looks a lot like WOMAN in the photo. MAN stares at her.)

YOUNG WOMAN: God sent you a visitor. Hello. That's some weather you have. I am soaked to the bone. Where can I hang my coat? On the rack? No, the water will drip on the floor. Where, then?..

(MAN is silent.)

YOUNG WOMAN: I'm sorry, is this a bad time?.. But the weather... I am wet and cold and I thought I may be able to wait out the rain in your house... Can you hear me?

(MAN does not respond. YOUNG WOMAN decides that the old man is deaf and raises her voice, gesturing with her hands.)

YOUNG WOMAN: I'm soaked and I would like to get warm and dry my things! Understand? He doesn't...
MAN *(quietly)*: I understand.

(MAN picks himself up.)

MAN: Come in, come in. You can hang your things to dry in the kitchen. No need to yell, I can hear you perfectly.
YOUNG WOMAN *(yells)*: Why then did you?!. Oops, why am I yelling if you can hear. I just need to get dry. But, if you don't mind, I'd spend the night.
MAN: Not at all. The more the merrier.
YOUNG WOMAN: What about the mistress of the house?
MAN *(quietly)*: I think I've heard it before. It already happened. My wife... she passed away ten years ago.

(MAN takes a tablecloth out of the dresser and puts it on the table.)

YOUNG WOMAN: Let me help.
MAN: Don't worry about it. You should change out of your wet clothes, or you'll catch a cold. You can wear this for now.

(MAN takes one of WOMAN's dresses out of the drawer.)

YOUNG WOMAN: Wonderful!

(YOUNG WOMAN exits.)
(MAN lays the table.)

MAN: Everything comes around. How everything comes around.

(YOUNG WOMAN returns wearing the dress from the photo. MAN is struck by the resemblance.)

MAN: This is impossible...

(Only MAN's lips are moving.)

MAN: How everything comes around...

YOUNG WOMAN: Now I can give you a hand. I am good at housekeeping.

(YOUNG WOMAN helps lay the table.)

YOUNG WOMAN: I cook well, too. One day, I...

(YOUNG WOMAN turns, bumps into the log, yelps.)

YOUNG WOMAN: Ouch. It'll give me a bruise! Why is this here?

(MAN does not respond).

YOUNG WOMAN: Do you hang your washing on it? What do you use it for?

(MAN, half dazed, shakes his head.)

YOUNG WOMAN: This log has to serve a purpose, since it's here.

(MAN gives no response.)

YOUNG WOMAN: Well, if you don't want to tell me, that's alright. Maybe it has a sentimental value for you?.. Alright, I'll drop the subject.

(YOUNG WOMAN sits on the chair. Silence. MAN stares at her. YOUNG WOMAN pretends not to notice and looks around the room. Finally, she can't bear it any longer.)

YOUNG WOMAN: Why do you stare at me like that? It makes me uncomfortable.

(MAN points at the photo)

MAN: Look.

(YOUNG WOMAN goes to the photo, studies it.)

YOUNG WOMAN: How strange...
MAN: That's why I've been staring at you.

(YOUNG WOMAN searches for the mirror, goes to it, studies her reflection with wonder, glances at the photo again.)

YOUNG WOMAN: Fancy that! It must be hard for you to see me.
MAN: Oh no, quite the opposite. I enjoy looking at you. It's as if the past twenty years never happened. It's all as it was back then. But not all...

Scene 5

(There is another chair on stage.)

(YOUNG WOMAN stands next to the log.)

YOUNG WOMAN: I simply do not understand. I just can't. Why should an object that serves no purpose, exist? What is it for? Can you get by without it?

(MAN is silent.)

YOUNG WOMAN: No? Tell me, can you live without it?

(MAN shrugs.)

MAN: I used to.
YOUNG WOMAN: And now? I understand sentimental memories. Is that it? Is there any other reason?

(MAN does not respond.)

YOUNG WOMAN: Alright, it can stay. But we need to find a use for it. What did you use it for before?
MAN: I'm not sure. I was told the house would collapse without it.
YOUNG WOMAN: Really? What nonsense.

MAN *(quietly)*: Nonsense indeed.

YOUNG WOMAN: Let's just cut off the part that sticks out, to make it level with other logs.

MAN *(repeats automatically)*: Just cut it off, even with the others.

YOUNG WOMAN: That's it. I don't understand. Why have you never thought about it? It's simple.

MAN *(quietly)*: Never thought about it. Simple.

YOUNG WOMAN: Fetch the saw. We'll do it right now.

MAN: The saw, yes. Don't you think the house could really collapse?

YOUNG WOMAN: If your house is built so stupidly, let it fall!

MAN *(quietly)*: Let it fall.

YOUNG WOMAN *(consolingly)*: The house will stand, don't worry. We won't remove the log. We'll just cut it.

MAN: I am old. I'm set in my ways. Besides... it's not proper to change the rules set before our time.

YOUNG WOMAN: Why not? What are you waiting for? Sooner or later, someone will...

MAN: Someone, but not you and I.

YOUNG WOMAN: What difference does it make? It will happen. Your log will be tossed in the dumpster or used as firewood.

MAN: It will be replaced with another.

YOUNG WOMAN: A useful one that will plug the hole and won't be in the way.

MAN: I know the house won't fall down without it. I have already tried. Watch.

(MAN goes to the log, loosens it, pulls it out of the wall with an effort, sets it on the floor, breathing heavily. YOUNG WOMAN helps MAN into the next room.)

Scene 6

(It's night. YOUNG WOMAN walks in slowly, exhausted. She removes one of the chairs; comes back, picks up the log and struggles to put it back into the wall; goes to the coat rack, puts on her coat, and leaves.)

(Rain is tapping on the roof. Suddenly the front door opens and TWO wet FIGURES in hooded coats enter. Their faces are shadowed. One is carrying a SUITCASE.)

FIGURE WITH the SUITCASE: There's nobody here. We can rest. Come in.

(FIGURE WITH the SUITCASE bumps into the log.)

FIGURE WITH the SUITCASE: What is this here? Come give me a hand.

(TWO FIGURES pull the log out of the wall and toss it. They study the room. They open the suitcase. They take an object out of the suitcase. The object is wrapped in cloth. They unwrap it. It is either a portrait or an icon in a frame. They hang it over the hole in the wall. They reverently kneel in front of the painting and pray, their backs to the audience.)

(CURTAIN)

(THE END)

Two short stories
by Nechama Sirotina

They say an apple doesn't fall far from the tree. My parents were actors from a young age. I followed in their steps. Then, my mother Nechama "Nina" Sirotina began writing short stories. I followed her there also. She wrote in Yiddish and translated her writings into Russian, and I edited them.

Rehearsal

by Nechama Sirotina

Y ou think actors can be found only in a theater, don't you?
Not so. Everyone is a bit of an actor. My *Bobe* (grandmother) was no exception. She became an actress in her later
years.

Everyone knows that actors rehearse a lot before present-
ing a play to an audience. So it was that once *Bobe* also set up
a rehearsal.

During the hot summer months when the sun started baking
the world early in the morning, the shutters on the windows
in our village were closed to trap the night's cool air inside,
but golden rays still penetrated through the cracks and gaps to
play with the dust motes and light the meager interior of our
"mansions" with magic light.

As soon as Aunt Elka, *Bobe*'s younger daughter, left for field
work at a Jewish collective farm (those did exist at the time),
Bobe quickly got out of bed, went to the dresser, and opened
a drawer. She took out a white bundle, unwrapped it, dropped
her nightgown to the floor, and put on... a white burial shroud.
She had long kept it in a bundle in the dresser. All in white,
Bobe walked from one window to the next, looking at her reflection in the dark glass and turning as if in a strange last
dance. She danced for a long time. Then, she lay down on the
floor and remained dead still, with a peaceful smile on her
face. Obviously, she was very content, so she lay like that for
a long time, unmoving.

Just then, having forgotten something at home, Aunt Elka returned. She opened the door and saw a body in white on

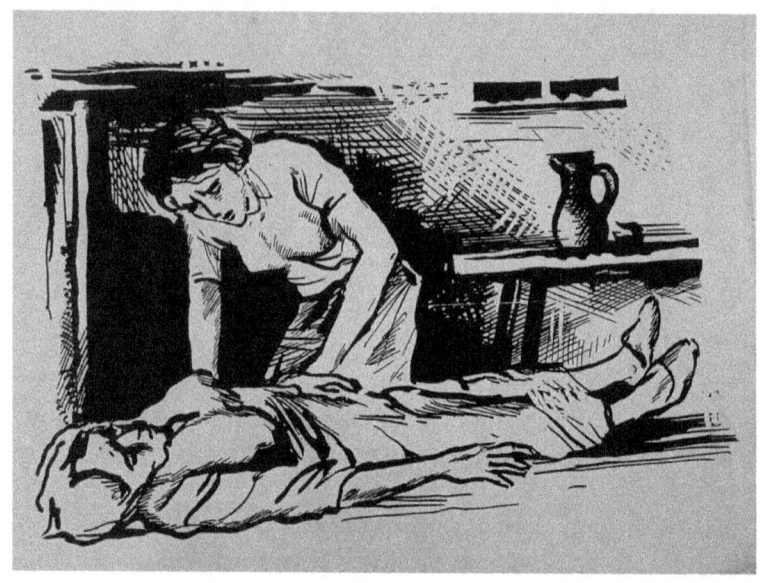

Artist Mikhail Turovsky

the floor in the middle of the room. In the dim light she could not tell who it was and was horrified to see a dead body in her home.

"*Vey iz mir!*" she cried in a voice that did not sound human.

Then, as every one of us would in such a situation, she called for her mother: "*Mame! Mame!* Where are you? Come quick! *Oy! Oy Mame!..*"

She was so scared she could not move. Her legs weakened, her knees buckled; she fell on her knees and only then saw that the body was her mother herself! That's when Aunt Elka really freaked out. She wailed so loud that the entire street could hear; she hugged her mother's body and, cradling it, wept.

Bobe, for her part, either surprised by her daughter's sudden reappearance or scared by her screaming, lay as if really dead; she couldn't either take a breath or move a muscle.

"*Oy teyere Mame!*" Aunt Elka wailed. "Why have you abandoned us?! Have we not loved you? Now we are poor orphans! What have you done?! Oy, *Mame* is dead!"

Aunt Elka, gathering momentum, was about to start pulling her hair out, when *Bobe* opened her eyes. Aunt Elka jumped on her feet and screamed: "Aaaaahhhh! Help me!"

"Shush, shush! What are you screaming for?" said *Bobe* calmly and sat up. "Don't you see I am alive and haven't died yet? I was just... rehearsing."

You may ask how I know all this. It's easy. I often spent nights at *Bobe*'s. That particular night I slept on top of the woodstove. In the morning, with bated breath, I watched *Bobe*'s "rehearsal" from under my colorful quilted blanket.

Bobe Plays Her Part

by Nechama Sirotina

The World War II was on. *Bobe*, most of her kin scattered on the roads of refugees, with just one of her many daughters, Elka, and her young granddaughter, Zisel, found shelter in a snowed-in village near the city of Orenburg at the southern end of the Ural mountains.

Winters are long and cold there, with piercing winds and snowstorms.

Having fled their *shletl* in Belarus in a hurry, the women did not bring any warm clothes. They believed that their travels wouldn't last long and that they would soon return home and resume their normal life. They even left their house in perfect order, a joy to come back to: everything was in place, the floor was thoroughly scrubbed, the shutters closed, the gate locked. They had enough time to do all that. But they never thought to bring winter clothing. It was, in a way, understandable: they left Belarus during warm, sunny days.

Still, *Bobe* remembered to bring two things: the white shroud and a huge man's sheepskin coat that her oldest grandson, Boruch, had left with her. Before going to war, Boruch dropped in to say goodbye to his *Bobe*.

"Here, *Bobenu*, this is for you," he said and put his coat on the bench. "You may need it. Who knows... You could maybe sell it... Or just keep it in remembrance of me, if... It's war, after all."

We all loved our kind old *Bobe* dearly. She had eleven grandchildren and four great-grandchildren, blessings be on her and us.

Artist Mikhail Turovsky

The war stretched into many hungry years. *Bobe* would not return home to hug her grandchildren and great-grand-children...

Bobe was seventy-nine. She had worked hard her entire life, meekly enduring all troubles and hardship. Her husband, my *Zeyde* (grandfather), was a severe man, even tyrannical. He was disabled — he was missing a leg and walked on crutches. He obeyed the Jewish law strictly and poured over the Holy Book all day. Housework, livestock, raising children, and breadwinning was laid on *Bobe*'s fragile shoulders. They had six children — five daughters and a son. Back in the day, daughters were generally a burden. So it was in this family. One of the daughters fell in love with a Ukrainian man and eloped with him to Chernihiv. Another daughter, a nurse, went to Poland. Perhaps these girls did not want to spend the rest of their lives in a poor God-forsaken *shletl*. *Zeyde*, of course, cursed them; he could not bear the shame and soon died of anxiety. *Bobe*, as a mother, bore everything and lived through everything. When the first daughter repented and returned from Cherni-hiv to the *shletl*, Babushka tried to hide her from the wrath of the neighbors, but failed, and soon the prodigal daughter was stoned by the Jews.

"Behold the sinner!" they screamed. "Be damned! Betrayer!"

The Belarusians did not approve of apostasy, either. They shook sticks at her and sent curses her way: "She ought to be killed!"

I heard it all from *Bobe*. I can still hear her warm, quiet voice. We, the grandchildren, were eager to hear these stories, and we wept for *Bobe*'s daughters — our aunts. *Bobe* herself never cried. There was sorrow in her eyes and her voice reflected the deep ache in her heart, but there were no tears.

I have gone down the rabbit hole of my distant childhood memories. Let's go back to *Bobe*'s last days.

She, her youngest daughter and her granddaughter lived in an old shed converted to living quarters. *Bobe* walked far into the forest for firewood, picked as much as she could and dragged it home. They didn't even own a sled. Aunt Elka got a job in a collective farm in the neighboring village. Elka got up before first light and came home after dark, dead on her feet. They had just enough food not to starve. It was not good for their health. On top of that, homesickness and missing her children undermined *Bobe*'s health. She lost weight and seemed to shrink with every passing hour.

One cold winter night a strong snowstorm hit. The wind raged, howled, and rattled the roof. Something in the chimney screamed in many terrible voices. *Bobe* lay on top of the stove where it was warm, but she still shivered and her teeth chattered.

"*Elke, Elke!*" *Bobe* called. "I am cold. Cover me with Boruch's coat."

Elka hurried to obey. *Bobe* got warm and fell asleep. At dawn, she woke up. She looked around the shed with her kind, intelligent eyes, as if saying goodbye. Her gaze lingered on her sleeping granddaughter.

"*Elke*, take care of her."

Then *Bobe* climbed off the stove and went outside. Soon she returned and washed her hands. Whispering something that must have been a prayer, she climbed back on her stove bed. Then she called for Elka: "Daughter, I am dying. Do not scream or weep, like you did at my 'rehearsal'. There is nothing you can do."

Bobe smiled with a corner of her mouth and continued: "Life is like theater. I have played my part. The end. Curtain falls. You are to keep playing. Remember to tell everything to my granddaughter *Nechamele*, my Moscow actress. Maybe she can use it for her roles. Now, put the shroud on me."

She said a prayer, sobbed several times, sighed deeply... and went out like a candle.

Burying her was hard work. There were no men in the village. Women gathered and carried *Bobe* to the cemetery. There are cemeteries everywhere... They could not dig a grave. The dirt was frozen and hard as rock. What could exhausted, weak women do? Fortunately, just then a dead old peasant was brought from another village by two old men and a legless soldier. Together, they managed to dig a common grave. Nobody had the strength to dig two. So, a Russian peasant and a Jewish refugee woman in a white shroud were laid to rest together.

The last thing Elka could do for *Bobe* was swaddle her body in Boruch's sheepskin coat to keep her warm.

So ends the sad tale of my grandmother.

Disclaimer

The views expressed by the author do not necessarily reflect the author's views. The author takes no responsibility for this publication.

www.ingramcontent.com/pod-product-compliance
Lightning Source LLC
Chambersburg PA
CBHW050408030726
47503CB00006B/2088